THE LAST DAI'AKAN

BOOK ONE OF THE OTAI CYCLE

JEREMY D. MILLER

Books to Hook
PUBLISHING

CONTENTS

First Edition: May 2023

ISBN 978-1-960207-72-2 (paperback)

Published by Books to Hook Publishing, LLC.

www.BooksToHook.com

For Margarita
For my daughter, Iliana

IN MEMORIAM
Victor Milan
The smartest person on Jupiter

PROLOGUE

They crossed from forest to desert in the blink of an eye. One moment the mule cart was speeding along a hard-packed road. The next, the wheels were churning through soft sand. Cactus walls the height of a man rose on both sides, twisted and bristling with spines. Codbaine pulled back on the reins, and the old mule dutifully stopped. He took his hat off and wiped his brow with his sleeve. His gaze shifted beyond where the path turned and disappeared from view, up to Aatma's pyramid shimmering in the distance, one side blown out. A gaping maw with three stone pillars marked the entrance.

"That's ominous," Bruno said, then spat into the dust. The tobacco-stained glob stuck to the ground like a beetle clinging to a rock, sparkling and still in the fierce light. He arched a brow in Codbaine's direction. Codbaine turned and held his gaze. The wind kicked up behind them as if sensing the moment. Bruno broke into a grin, and they laughed.

For as long as Codbaine could remember, Aatma's dungeon had stood in the middle of the forest on the outskirts of Traveston, carved from stone and impenetrable, manufacturing in the dark arts for the Empress and killing adventurers who dared to explore its depths. That all changed when several clans came together and successfully destroyed the dungeon. Codbaine had seen the parade of adventurers with their sparkling armor and array of potions and weapons strutting into town and announcing their plans to sack the dungeon. Healthy wagers had been placed on how many would survive. Codbaine himself had put a shiny silver mark on no survivors. The payout was low, but he thought it easy money. For all the adventurers' bluster, the villagers didn't have high hopes. He had been shocked in the morning when his youngest daughter, Eliza, had woken him up with an envelope from the Scavenger Guild flapping in her hand announcing the dungeon's defeat and Codbaine's first scavenger rights.

He returned his attention to the cactus walls in front of him. Legend had it that a single prick could kill a full-grown horse, much less a mule like Dhor. Codbaine had no interest in testing the legend's veracity, even with the energy core out. He gave a flick of the reins and guided the mule forward.

"I like some of them plants," Bruno said, pointing to a stalk full of yellow flowers sticking out of a nest of interlaced leaves. "Maybe they'd be worth something?"

Bruno could out-dig anyone, and he was a dear friend, but the man had a way of ferreting out the least valuable objects on a given job, and this job was not only close to home but potentially very lucrative.

"Maybe," Codbaine said with a sideways glance. "Let's see what awaits us nearer to the dungeon. There's no sense in digging for treasure when there's plenty in plain view."

Bruno shrugged and spat.

Codbaine was eager to reach the entrance. He wasn't worried about the adventurers. There was only so much they could have carted off if they bothered to take anything. The real money was in the memory crystals. People would be buying those crystals and replaying the invasion for years. The guild tax alone would provide a fortune to the survivors. No, Codbaine was more worried about other scavengers. They'd be along soon enough.

Dhor stayed squarely in the center of the path, clear of the cactus on either side, pulling the two of them and the empty cart without difficulty. His ears twitched at the bothersome insects. The serpentine route took more than an hour to navigate, and as they grew closer to the pyramid, great rents in the ground and cactus walls became more frequent, with pieces of shiny carapaces shimmering red and green in the light. Chunks of flesh-eating worms as thick as his leg were strewn about in pools of blood. He had to give it to the clans: they lived up to their claims. He wondered if the Empress's guards could have won such a victory. Codbaine banished the blasphemous thought from his head and gave Bruno a stern look, fearing that his friend could somehow read his thoughts, but Bruno was busy studying the carnage.

The cactus slowly receded, and sand was replaced with stone. The sound of Dhor's hooves clip-clopping mixed with the light howl of the wind at the dungeon's towering entrance. Codbaine and Bruno pulled their handkerchiefs over their noses and scanned the bloodbath around them. A horde of zombies lay dismembered on the stone floor, along with lycanthropes, serpents, scorpions, and spiders.

"Grab the pincers, fangs, and stingers first," Codbaine said. "The apothecaries will pay good money for those. I'm going in to have a look."

Bruno hopped off the wagon, pulled out a skinning knife, and went to work while Codbaine grabbed a new torch from the back of the cart and lit it.

Inside the pyramid, the fetid air hung thick. The grand hall was full of the dead, minions dismembered and piled up to either side, while the dungeon's flesh peeled away from the walls and floor, blackened and brittle. Even with his handkerchief over his face, Codbaine had to breathe through his mouth to keep from retching. He could see some Haqi script sparsely covering what remained of the dungeon skin, pale and lifeless, devoid of energy. Codbaine passed through the hall and a large room before arriving at a broad stone bridge as thick as he was tall. He noted a few smears of blood across the rock as he crossed the gap and peered over the side. The torchlight barely penetrated the darkness. It wasn't hard to imagine where the dead had gone during the fight across the gap.

On the other side of the bridge, he passed through several more rooms, each full of tables covered with books, measuring devices, flasks, and containers of chemicals and powders. Much of the equipment lining the walls was destroyed, but some appeared salvageable. Human bodies littered the floor in these rooms: alchemists, scribes, apothecaries, assistants, and other members of the dark arts. There was money to be had in these rooms, but space was valuable on the mule cart, and Codbaine had been burned before on thinking a particular book or piece of machinery was valuable. Guessing could cost him dearly. His eye was attuned to the more simplistic: jewelry, weapons, essential potion ingredients, anything that could be sold quickly for cash.

When Codbaine arrived at the main hall, he first noticed the throne in the distance and the headless person sitting on it. A jolt of fear shot up his spine, and he ducked behind a shiny object. Golden scales glittered in the torchlight. Codbaine thought of a fish and reached out to touch the scales. They broke away and stuck to his hand. He moved his torch to the right and stared into a lifeless eye the size of a boulder. *A golden dragon!* It had been killed in the final battle. He remained frozen, staring at his reflection in the eye until he recognized the frightened man staring back. *You idiot.*

He took a deep breath, and his fear thawed enough for him to regain his purpose. He stood tall and mumbled to himself, annoyed at his cowardice, before stepping around the great carcass of the dragon and continuing forward. His torchlight illuminated the gruesome scene as he drew closer to the throne on the opposite side of the room. Slumped to one side, the corpulent body of the dark lord was covered in a thick cloak with a stump and a dark stain around the cloth at the neck where the head had been. Pieces of flesh and blood sat at the corpse's feet, remains of his once great army. Codbaine shook his head. *This is what I was afraid of?* He turned in a circle and took in the large, lifeless room, thinking of the battle that must have happened. He couldn't wait to purchase the memory crystal. The clans would soon pass into legend. Codbaine felt pride at being the first to gaze upon their triumphant deeds. He swung his torch back and forth, fighting off imaginary monsters, then turned to the headless body on the throne and brought his torch across the neckline in an arc as if he had been the one doing the beheading.

"You, Aatma, have been vanquished," he announced. "Nothing to say, then?" Codbaine nodded his approval at the corpse's silence and paced back and forth. "Serves you right. A plague, a scourge you've been on our lands for all these years. No longer! The heroic Codbaine has made quick work of you and your pet dragon. Your crown is no more. You got too greedy, taking advantage of Empress Inalda, minting coin off the dead of her army...."

Codbaine stopped in his tracks, a glint catching his eye. He hopped up to the throne in one motion and pulled back the sleeve of one hand, revealing a ruby ring sparkling on the pinky finger. Codbaine gave a shout of glee, lifted the hand, and spat on the finger, then worked the ring back and forth until he pulled it off. He held it close to the torch and examined the gemstone, a ruby the size of his index fingernail was held in place by four golden prongs. Codbaine frowned when he noticed the black dots speckling the jewel and covering tiny Haqi symbols. The ring was heavy. He recognized the exquisite craftsmanship and knew the ring would bring a small fortune even with a ruined gem.

Codbaine tucked it away and examined the body thoroughly before exploring the rest of the room. He collected several daggers and two potions that had survived the battle, likely because of their thick flasks. He put them all in a bag and bowed to the headless corpse on the throne with a flourish.

"The Scavenger Guild thanks you for your service," Codbaine said. He spun on his heels and returned to plunder some valuables he had spotted on the way in.

The sun was past its zenith when Codbaine finished his third trip through the dungeon and emerged from the entrance. A dust trail kicked up in the distance. He shielded his eyes with a hand and saw a wagon train working along the path. Other scavengers were coming. He stripped cloth from the dead minion next to him, a lycanthrope with its snout ripped from its face, and wrapped several glass flasks he had found and placed them neatly in the cart. He was about to shout at Bruno when his friend emerged from around the pyramid's corner.

"I found two minions," Bruno said.

Codbaine looked at the entrance, then to Bruno, contemplating whether to go back in or investigate with Bruno. "What kind?" he asked.

"A succubus and a zombie."

Two of the lowest creatures possible, Codbaine thought,

although the succubus could be worth something to the right buyer. "We're better off harvesting materials out of the dungeon. It'd be more valuable, and we don't have enough room in the cart for two minions." He pointed to the wagons in the distance. "Besides, we are running out of time."

Bruno glanced at the wagons approaching, then spat before strolling to the cart and looking in. "We can take one and slide it in the side here," he said, "to stabilize and protect the jars."

Codbaine was about to say they could strip the clothes from some of the minions and pack the jars in, but he saw the look of determination in Bruno's eyes and knew his fellow scavenger had all but made up his mind. It wasn't often you could get minions free and clear without help from the Summoning Guild. However, the condition was everything when it came to value. No one wanted a crippled minion sucking up energy when it was reanimated. He glanced at the wagon. "We might be able to fit the succubus. Let's take the cart over and have a look."

The two bodies lay face up on the desert floor near a far corner of the pyramid. Codbaine hopped off the cart and examined them. "Help me," Codbaine said as they flipped the bodies over.

The succubus was a mess. Her dark hair was tangled and mixed with sand, while a stained dress covered an emaciated body. She had seen many battles and may have been beautiful once, but Codbaine wouldn't have wagered on it. Her nose looked like it had been broken several times and was slanted to one side, while her face was scarred from claw marks. One of her wings had a large hole in it. There's no way she could fly. Dried blood crusted her mouth. Codbaine leaned over and lifted her lip, exposing broken, jagged teeth. He shook his head.

"She won't heal right, even with an energy core pumping her with energy. It's been too long," Codbaine said.

Bruno grunted, and they walked over to the zombie. If the succubus looked in rough shape, the zombie was a downright disaster. It lay in its blood, skin a sickly green hue mottled with black and brown splotches. The zombie's right leg was broken at the knee and twisted out. Even the beheaded corpse of the dark lord was less repulsive.

Codbaine looked back and forth between the minions and scratched his head. "If I had to choose one, and I'm not saying we have to, I'd say let's...."

"Take the zombie," Bruno interrupted.

"What?" Codbaine said in disbelief. "You want to take the zombie? That creature over there," he said, pointing exaggeratedly to the minion on the ground. "The one that's bleeding out with a broken leg? It'll die before we can put it in suspension. The succubus is the better choice."

"We could bring it to one of the healers. If we can only fit one, it should be the zombie."

"He ain't worth anything, Bruno. And he's going to leak all over the place. How about we grab one of those plants you were so fond of on the way out?"

"We take him," Bruno said. "The succubus will live longer, and we can tell the scavengers coming in about her."

Codbaine rolled his eyes. "I can never understand why you want to save these pathetic creatures. Remember the squirrel when we were kids? The damn thing couldn't even walk."

Bruno shrugged. "We've got the room and all the money we need," he said. "No reason the creature has to die out here alone. Ain't right."

"He's not alone. If we leave them both, they'll die together. Or maybe we can tell the incoming scavengers about them?"

Bruno shook his head. "We take the zombie," he said.

"All right, all right," Codbaine conceded. "You know, you would have made a lousy adventurer."

"That's why I'm here with you," Bruno said with a fake smile.

They waited at the entrance for the new scavengers to arrive so they could have the path to themselves going out. Bruno mentioned the succubus to the first group but was otherwise silent. No good could come from flaunting your gains.

When they hit the tree line, Codbaine took a final look back at the pyramid and then at the contents of their cart. It was an admirable haul, even with the zombie lying on its side propped up against the cart wall. The minion had made decent packing material, keeping the jars from tilting as Dhor trudged through the soft sand. He passed his hand over the ring in his pocket. They would feast that night, and he would buy Eliza a new dress at a good shop in the morning.

Kingdoms are ruled with a quill, not a sword, Empress Inalda thought, shaking the stiffness from her hand. She gave her finance minister a wary eye when he reached for another paper and put it on her desk.

"This is a title of nobility for Agon Letcher. He fought on the Kandar border against the outlanders and single-handedly killed a dozen men before collapsing from exhaustion. He was given a parade upon returning to the Capital."

"Any truth to it? No, never mind. I don't care." The Empress scanned the document and saw that the bequeathed estate was in the countryside. She signed it. Fatini gave a curt nod and removed the paper, placing it on the stack. He was reaching for another piece when a knock came at the door.

The wiry man turned in his seat, the paper wavering in his still hand.

"Who is it?" Inalda asked. She tried to keep her voice steady, but her hand was cramping and tired.

Her guardsman answered, "Zeniah is here, Empress. She states it is urgent."

Fatini turned back with a frown.

"We must continue the signings at a later date, Fatini." Inalda felt her spirits lift.

He nodded, then gathered up the pile of documents and left.

"Let her through," she announced.

Zeniah curtsied and took Fatini's vacated seat with the Empress's permission. It was an uncommon sight to see Zeniah in such disarray. Her gray bun was slightly crooked with wisps of hair poking out, and she was breathing heavily as if she had run up a flight of stairs. The Empress was about to say something when Zeniah spoke.

"Aatma's dungeon has fallen, Empress."

Inalda hissed, receiving the news like a slap in the face. She closed her eyes and took several deep breaths. The catastrophic consequences of her troops pushing into the outlands without the necessary enhancements raced through her mind. *Not now,* she chastised herself; *stay in the present, damn you.* "When did this happen? Who did it?"

"Two days past. Multiple elite clans out of the Adventurer's Guild led the raid. They suffered heavy losses. The guilds have not yet released the memory crystal, but my sources tell me it is imminent."

"And the world will know my leading supplier has been destroyed, and my forces will be vulnerable. Elite, indeed," Inalda scoffed, "Aatma's defenses were unparalleled. How often have we seen clans get wiped out before making it to the entrance?"

"More than I can count, Empress. Do you think they acted alone?"

"Or what? That the guild acted against me? The outcome is the same. They will get rich on the spoils and entertain the masses. Meanwhile, a surge of dungeons will struggle to replace what I have lost. The damage is done. Our lines will buckle when the news spreads to the troops and beyond. We will have lost the advantage I have spent the last decade building."

"What is there to do?"

"Let that be my worry. You have done well to get this news to me." Her mistress of information grimaced. "Anything else?" Empress Inalda held her breath and exhaled when Zeniah shook her head. "Tell the guardsman I want to speak to Ma'Toli."

Zeniah's face paled. "Yes, my Empress."

Empress Inalda canceled her appointments for the morning and met with her war council. The generals sat before her stone-faced as they listened to the news of Aatma's demise. In return, the Empress heard their war projections without Aatma's potent enhancers. Collapse without a large influx of troops within months was the short of it. The meeting put her in a sour mood, and she excused herself happily when word of Ma'Toli's arrival reached her ears. Before she left, she let the generals know that contingency plans should be generated for their meeting the following week.

The old mage sat in the chair opposite her desk with his two hands propped on the handle of his cane. He did not look at the Empress when she walked in but waited for her to come into his view before speaking.

"You have come," she said.

Ma'Toli arched an eyebrow. His gaunt frame should have looked ludicrous in the red pomp of the High Mage, but he somehow managed to look respectful.

"I may be five times your age, but I still come when my Empress demands it."

"I thank you."

The old man nodded and remained silent.

"My need is great. Aatma has fallen, and with him, my chances of pushing into the outlands to produce more otai." Her kingdom ran on otai, and its flow had dwindled in recent years. The Mage Guild had to feel the pain. "I stand to lose a great deal. As do you. With Aatma's enhancements, a tent group in my army could hold against thrice their numbers. Our advantage has always been with the Great Game. Aatma's downfall is our downfall."

"I have heard those words many times, Empress. Old and new dungeon masters alike will scramble to take his place. There will be others like Aatma, and you will find a way to survive just as you and your line always have."

Inalda gripped her chair, her lips pursed, "I feel like I'm being squeezed between the guilds, the Great Game, and our need for more resources. I grow weary of just surviving. I want to flourish." Inalda did nothing to wipe away the tears streaming down her cheeks. "Is there nothing you can do to help me, Ma'Toli?"

Ma'Toli sat for a long while in his chair, looking around at the portraits of her family members, then met her gaze. He was a heap of wrinkles covered in white hair, but his eyes glowed like the waters of a lagoon at midday. "There is a way. A way to get enough otai to fuel your needs and ours. But it is danger-ous. We may pay for it with our lives."

"You will not die, Ma'Toli. Your power is great."

Ma'Toli shook his head. "Nonsense, everyone dies. I will

tell you of one of my brothers with greater power who lost his way and let you decide whether your salvation or doom lies in his undoing."

Empress Inalda listened and feared the choice she had to make.

CHAPTER ONE

Talia waded into the lagoon, and the nausea that had haunted her these long months abated. Her hands worked mechanically, tying her lengthy, black hair into a bun as she sunk into the calm waters. She stretched her arms and turned to regard Mount Laiya in the dying light. The mountain loomed over her, its lichen and moss-covered crags no longer discernible. She searched for the glow of her father's staff.

This is forbidden. Talia felt the warmth rise in her cheeks with the memory of her mother's admonishment and turned her gaze from the mountainside.

She had snuck onto the roof of their hut as a child to watch the Dai'akan leave on pilgrimage. That was before her father had been named the replacement. Her mother, Palani, always seeming to know when Talia was up to no good, walked out of the hut with her hands on her hips, turned, and looked right at her.

"Get down from there, child."

Talia remembered feeling surprised and ashamed when

she scurried across the bounded thatch and jumped down in front of her mother, her head hanging low.

"Do not meddle in that which you cannot comprehend."

"I wasn't meddling, Mother. I was watching. How else am I to learn?"

"What you do—watching the Dai'akan on his journey—is forbidden."

"Why?"

"The Dai'akan is performing a great service. He must focus on his pilgrimage. If he sensed our worry, it could interfere with his concentration, with his journey to see Pa'vil. The Dai'akan must be free of terrestrial burden to serve the divine. Seek guidance and forgiveness from Pa'vil before you sleep this night."

Talia was about to ask how Pa'vil could hear her speak and what precisely the Dai'akan's job was, but her mother's expression made it plain that there would be no further discussion on the topic. Talia had returned to her bed and lain awake into the night, wondering what was at the top of the mountain. She even attempted to talk to Pa'vil but received no answer. Her worry and curiosity were only magnified when the Dai'akan died later that season.

She floated on her back with her arms swirling at her sides and sprayed water across her protruding stomach with a flick of her wrist. She felt movement. *Your child grows restless, Kol'val.* She put a hand on her stomach and attempted a deep breath— a kick in the ribs was her reward. *Ioane was right. You are a defiant one.*

Ioane, her godmother and leader of the elder's council, was a wisp of a woman with white hair down to her knees. She was also the oldest person in Arutua. Before Talia knew of her pregnancy, Ioane had laid hands on her as they weaved *kaftwa* and told of a fire of spirit brewing in her belly that would change the world. Talia thought of Kol'val's excitement when she'd told him of Ioane's foretelling later that night. "He will do many things with that fire," Kol'val had said. "Yes, *she* will," Talia had replied.

She felt another kick. *Be patient, little one. Kol'val will see you enter this world. Pa'vil will guide him home true.*

Talia let her mind drift and then focused on the constellation above her; Manoa, the young warrior heroically poised with one hand holding the head of the slain water dragon, Amakua, and a sword in the other. He gained fame and wealth in his adventures, only to lose it all when he fell in love with a spirit and went mad chasing it across the world. Only in his death were they joined. She began recounting the stories of other constellations as she spotted them; Leinani and Hamina, the twin sisters wrapped in a triumphant embrace after they tricked the malevolent Niuhana out of marriage; Rua playing dice against the serpent Aimata for passage out of the underworld; Kehau the coward fleeing his throng of unruly children who would eventually catch and eat him.

She did not know how much time had passed when she decided to swim to the shore and return to her village. Lit by starlight, the path was narrow and weaved through thick grass. She could have walked it with her eyes closed and was lost in thought when she entered the outskirts of the village. A rush of warm, briny air hit her as she descended the gentle slope. Arutua lay before her, a series of steeply pitched, circular huts elevated on stilts forming a circle around a large, rectangular building belonging to the elder's council. Beyond the buildings, a path led to a sandy beach where a long row of canoes sat. The village was dark save for a few flickering lights.

Talia approached her family's hut near the outskirts of the village, a thatched cone sitting on top of mature bamboo scaffolding lashed with woven reeds. The interior was simple, a large room with mats on one side for sleeping and a square table and chairs on the other for eating. Her father had made the table and chairs when Talia was a child.

Palani greeted Talia and sat opposite her at the table. She cupped Talia's face and smiled warmly before pouring tea.

"Kava leaf to calm the wild spirit growing within," she said. "How was the water?"

Talia tried not to groan as she shifted in her seat. "The warm waters greeted me with open arms, but the little one did not appreciate it as much. I'm sore from all the kicking." She took a sip of her tea and rubbed her side.

"They will kick. Most of the time, they need not have a reason."

"Perhaps the baby misses her father?" She added, startled at the emotion in her voice.

"Kol'val will be here, my child. You need not worry about that."

Her mother sat up and leaned forward, kissing Talia on the forehead. Talia felt a tightness in her chest loosen.

"What of the festival preparations?" She asked, changing the subject.

Palani returned to her seat. "I was out late today harvesting arrowroot and yams. Tomorrow will be a long day, but we will be ready. Pa'vil willing."

The Tau'lai festival signaled the celebration of Pa'vil coming down from the heavens and giving life to his people from his flesh. It marked the beginning of the harvest season with a feast and a series of dances. The elder council had elected her mother to organize the festival, a big responsibility and a position of high honor amongst their people. Talia's participation would be limited as even watered-down otai, the nectar of Pa'vil, was forbidden during pregnancy.

Palani continued talking about the festival—building the

bonfire, gathering the remaining food, and setting up the dance. Talia sat silently and enjoyed her tea and her mother's soothing voice. Before long, exhaustion settled in. She put aside her empty cup and prepared for sleep. As she lay on the mat and felt her eyelids close, she said, "I couldn't help but look for him, Mother. Forgive me. May Pa'vil guide Father on his journey."

"Sleep," Palani replied, "the Dai'akan will find his way."

THE SUN BEAT at Masima's back, and sweat stung his eyes. He shuffled across the ledge. A loud crack echoed as the rock broke under his weight. His feet flailed and scraped against the mountainside while his hands strained under his weight. The pounding of blood filled his ears. He imagined himself tumbling down the mountainside smashing into the rock below. His foot found purchase, just enough to take some of his weight. The sharpness of the edge bit through his leather sandal. He grimaced and pushed off with his toe while pulling himself upward. Moving quickly with adrenaline, he traversed across the last of the wall before hoisting himself onto a narrow path. Masima flipped over on the ground and took large gulps of air. His muscles felt like water. *Too close.* He sat up, removed his pack, and took out a canteen and a cloth bag of fried breadfruit. While eating and drinking, he took the opportunity to take off his shoe and examine his bruised toenail.

I may lose it—a small price to pay for my life.

So thirsty. Pa'vil's thought came into Masima's mind. He put the shoe back on and got to his feet, brushing himself off.

I'm coming. Masima pushed the thought to the edge of his consciousness and let it slip into the abyss. He had studied the diaries of the previous Dai'akans after being selected. Each of his predecessors had added their thoughts on how best to communicate with Pa'vil, so Masima had a notion of what to expect, but there was no way one could know. How do you explain vision to a man without sight? He would sound mad. He remembered mixing their blood before the first feeding, then Pa'vil was just there, a vast power waiting beyond some unseen barrier, sending him a cascade of thoughts and images of events long past.

Maybe I am mad.

Masima untied his staff from his pack, hefting it in one hand. Made from smooth ebony wood and engraved with Haqi symbols, the staff was capped with a green orb that glowed with the darkness, making night ascension possible. It was incredibly sturdy and had saved Masima on more than one occasion. Some of the previous Dai'akans had remarked on its durability in their diaries, calling it indestructible. Masima did not doubt the claim. He checked his dagger sheathed at his belt. Its pale, translucent hilt pulsed a soft emerald green in his shadow.

"Protect the dagger and staff at all costs," he recited, "for they make your journey and sacrifice possible."

He had found Kalani, his predecessor, on that first ascension of Mount Laiya. Ashen and cold, Kalani's body was slumped against the mountainside in a heap with the staff and dagger secured. Masima had wept for Kalani, then—for the memories of them playing in the fields and exploring the island. Kalani was called to serve as the Dai'akan when Masima was not yet sixteen. *So long ago.* Arihi, the Dai'akan then, had been the only Dai'akan in Masima's lifetime not to die on Mount Laiya. Stumbling into Arutua in the early morning, incoherent and bleeding, he had died sometime during the day with the healers. Like everything else surrounding the

Dai'akan, his death was shrouded in secrecy. Kalani was raised to the position soon after.

Masima was thankful to Pa'vil for choosing one so strong, for Kalani served longer than any other Dai'akan. He remembered Kalani's look of awe and fear when he was called to the elders to test that morning. It had been unusual for the elders to pick one so young for a position of such great importance, which Masima could not have fully grasped at the time, but the elders had tested many of the males in the village. He had been happy for Kalani, even envious when he was chosen. That all changed when Masima took up the torch. He held a deep sorrow for Kalani, for the life that could have been. At least Masima had a family and an opportunity to live outside the narrow boundaries of servitude.

He continued around Mount Laiya on a well-worn path until it abruptly disappeared under a scree slope on the other side. He turned sharply and began the final ascent to the top. He used the staff as a stake, and his muscles burned with each step.

Feed me, child.

Masima did not answer this time, focusing on the task. He had read of a Dai'akan long past falling to his death. When he hadn't returned, a new Dai'akan was appointed, and he spent months searching for the body on Mount Laiya. While he searched, the vegetation on the island began to wilt, and people started to get sick. The returning traders even said they could see the island from afar as Pa'vil's protective shroud failed. By the time the new Dai'akan found the dagger and staff and fed Pa'vil, he was practically killed from repeat feedings; such was the god's thirst and ferocity. In the journal, the Dai'akan described Pa'vil's thoughts, violent ramblings about monsters chasing him in the dark, and lost love. It took years to stabilize Pa'vil and restore the island's health.

Pausing to catch his breath, Masima turned and looked down at the mountain's base, where a thin rim of black rock marked the lagoon. Talia was two when he first took her to swim in the lagoon. She would climb across the rocks on the far edge, each time a look of triumph painting her face, before catapulting herself into the water. She was fearless. He shifted his gaze towards Arutua and wondered what Palani and Talia were doing at that moment, no doubt preparing for the Tau'lai.

Kyra, my love? Are you there? You must go. I will come when I can.

Masima's smile faded when violent images and thoughts flooded in from Pa'vil.

A creature—Kyra was her name—with eyes the color of fire and smooth, alabaster skin reached out to him. A mouth opened, revealing rows of sharp teeth stained with blood.

I cannot save you, Kyra, my love. They know. You must run.

Raw terror dripped through the link. Masima shook his head, trying to banish the emotion and unwanted memories.

You are safe, Pa'vil. I am coming to feed you.

Masima struggled to take a mental picture of his view from Mount Laiya and pass it to Pa'vil. He communicated simple ideas without difficulty, but an image was complex, and he could never be sure if what he sent Pa'vil was received. He was not surprised when there was no answer.

The loose rock of the scree field gave way to hard-packed earth when Masima crested the edge that dropped down into the caldera. The caldera looked like a giant spoon had scooped it out, and its waters were a mixture of otai and rainwater. The aquamarine liquid glistened in the sun. An elevated path of rock led from where Masima stood to Pa'vil's resting place, a plain stone building on a moss-covered hill in the caldera's center.

Masima turned and looked back at the wisps of clouds slipping through the sky. Birds darted back and forth, their bodies making swishing noises as they danced in the wind. He remembered the tranquility he had first felt coming here after the horror of finding Kalani's body. If only he could find a way to revisit that sense of peace.

He stopped at the pool's edge and filled his empty water bag with otai, carefully keeping his hands dry. Some of the oldest journals detailed the dangers of handling the liquid after a feeding. It was best to fill the bag when you had your wits about you.

The green orb on the staff flared to life when he entered the stone building. A desiccated body lay on the slab in the middle. Parched skin stretched over bone.

You are here. Oh, you are here, my sweet bag of blood.

Masima set the staff against the wall and knelt beside Pa'vil.

I am here.

Be quick. I need more. You are all at risk. Only I can save you—more blood!

It is I, the same Dai'akan. Nothing has changed. The island is well. Your people are flourishing.

There was silence, then a series of curses. Violent images flooded Masima's mind.

I will get you one day, just like the bags before you. One day I will be free.

I am sorry to disappoint you, Pa'vil, the great protector of our people.

Pa'vil's body shook with a raspy wheeze. *Great protector or prisoner?*

Masima took his staff from the wall and laid it next to Pa'vil. He took Pa'vil's hand and wrapped it around the shaft. *Pa'vil, protector of this island, do you swear to drink only as much as you need to survive and not a drop more? Do you swear to preserve my life and health above all else?*

The staff's glow pulsed faster and brighter as Masima pushed the oath across his mind and into Pa'vil's consciousness.

I swear it.

The green light flared. Masima closed his eyes and turned away. When the light had died down to nothing more than a trickle, Masima removed the dagger. It radiated a vibrant green much as the staff had and cast Pa'vil in a ghoulish light. Masima made a horizontal incision in the palm of his hand, then took Pa'vil's hand and made a similar cut. The dagger hummed softly when it sliced through Pa'vil's mottled, gray skin. Masima sheathed the blade and joined their hands together palm to palm, his bright red blood mixed with the viscous black ooze of Pa'vil's. Masima felt a worm-like vessel probe his palm and then burrow into him. Their fingers interlocked into a tight ball. Pa'vil's eyes opened wide, shining a vibrant blue. The muscles of his face twitched momentarily as if relearning to move after a long period of disuse. The corners of his mouth crept up into a smile. A groan escaped Masima's lips, then quickly rose to a scream. His body was racked with pain as Pa'vil fed.

CHAPTER TWO

G abriel Shook stood before the weathered door, reading the white letters painted across its surface, *Dungeon Regear*. He glanced down the empty cobblestone street and shivered in the morning chill before taking the crinkled paper from his vest pocket and confirming his destination for the hundredth time. With a sigh, he opened the door and stepped in.

Beams of light filtering through the front windows struggled to illuminate sagging shelves filled with traps, ropes, boots, rocks, and sundry items Gabe didn't recognize. The mix of camphor and dust caused his eyes to water, and he pulled out his embroidered handkerchief and sneezed several times.

A high-pitched voice called from the dim recesses. "I'll be right there."

Gabe's finger passed over the ridges of the gold coin in his pocket, a ten-mark bearing Empress Inalda's profile, and he squinted, searching for the source of the voice. A pulsing blue orb emerged from the darkness and approached him as if to answer his probing gaze. Its frosted form, crisscrossed with translucent stripes, spun languidly in the open air, casting an eerie and ever-evolving whirl of lines on its surroundings. A banshee floated in the orb's wake and made a clicking noise. Her short hair fanned out around her as if submerged in water. Her sightless eyes were like black pearls embedded in a porcelain mask.

A Truvian Banshee, Gabe thought, how exotic. A list of pros and cons (mostly cons) popped into his head from his cryptozoology class. The Truvian Banshee was intelligent with excellent echolocation and could sense a creature's alignment within ten feet. They were susceptible to the elements, and while their screams could turn some adventurers mad and scare them off, they usually just angered other minions and sowed confusion. There were stories of their hair getting tangled up in some newly installed piece of equipment on a dungeon wall or screams of panic if their echolocation was compromised. They were impractical for the frontlines and better suited to working in a laboratory or—in this case—a shop.

"Welcome to Dungeon Regear. The consignment shop for all your dungeon needs. I am called Sara. How can I help you?"

"Yes, ahh, my name is Gabe. I require a minion...or two," he added. "For my new dungeon." Why was he trying to impress a minion? And who was he kidding? The markup at a consignment store would be horrendous. He'd be lucky to buy a rat, much less two minions. He struggled to keep his face void of emotion, then remembered he was talking to a blind minion.

"Come, we will show you our inventory," Sara said.

Gabe looked around expecting someone else but realized Sara included the orb in 'we.' A captured spirit, perhaps? He followed them past several aisles, glancing down each one with disinterest, before turning and walking to a pair of darkly stained doors. Etched across the doors was a carving of a doji that looked to be playing a musical instrument next to a pile of clothes.

"That is unusual," Gabe said. "I didn't know dojis could play the flute."

The clicking noise died with Sara's scowl. "It is a doji gnawing on a human leg next to its corpse—a warning to those who enter the store that these doors are off-limits without supervision. The master was quite clear with the enchanter about what he wanted."

Gabe took a step back and cocked his head to one side. "Of course, I see it now, what exquisite detail," he lied.

Sara turned back towards the doors and raised her hands. The orb lifted above her and began pulsing faster and brighter. Gears whirled in the doors with a low buzz followed by metallic clicks. The doors parted in silence, revealing blackness. The orb raced ahead, giving off sparks of blue light so that the vaulted room slowly came into view through a thousand sparkling droplets, each suspended in the air. Rows of transparent vats, each containing a minion submerged in pale liquid, filled the space.

I could repel adventurers with an army like this, buying precious time to fulfill guild contracts. I would grow rich, avenge my parents' death, and buy a cure for Miranda. The weight of the single coin in his pocket pulled him out of his fantasy and back into the large room, standing in front of the banshee and her orb.

"Are you listening?"

"Yes, listening, sure," he mumbled, moving his hands to the lapels of his jacket.

"The creatures are organized by price, increasing from left to right and from front to back. There are three prices on each tag in front of the vats with dates on the first two prices. If the date has passed, then refer to the next price. Each creature is suspended and preserved with a soporific spell. I am authorized to bind your minions to you. We will need your destination address and preferred delivery time if you wish to transfer them to your dungeon via teleportation. The transportation service adds 10% to the price. We require a vial of your blood for binding purposes."

The orb spun slowly in her hand as she talked.

"Please remember that we do not own these creatures. We are merely the intermediaries. These prices were set in the contract with the sellers. There is no bargaining or trading. The only currencies accepted are the Empress's coin, precious metals, or jewels. Do you understand and accept these terms?"

"I do," Gabe said. *So much for selling a share of future dungeon profits.*

"Just call out my name if you need anything. Again, my name is Sara."

When Gabe was alone, he walked to the nearest vat. A sinewy wolf covered in dark fur floated, its jaws agape in frozen rage. A tag dangled from a pole in front of the vat. Gabe picked it up and felt his stomach lurch. Fifty gold marks and the first two dates had already passed? This was as cheap as this minion would get. Gabe looked closely, and the front right leg ended in a stump. Who would buy a maimed wolf for that much? But Gabe knew the answer the minute the question popped into his head. There were strict rules when contracting a summoner to create a new minion. And while summoners were bound by confidentiality just like any other guild member, they were expensive and notoriously finicky in their inspections, giving black marks at the slightest perceived insult or reporting minor infractions. Buying a second-hand minion allowed for some flexibility and kept one less guild out of your business.

Gabe passed the large cats, serpents, and spiders until he reached the last row on the left, the cheapest minions. Floating before him, or more accurately, lying before him, was a splotchy half-skeleton with a missing arm. Its red eyes dimly glowed out of the liquid like two dying embers. Gabe couldn't bring himself to look down at the tag. Not yet, he thought. Instead, he walked past the next three vats, a zombie with a leg turned in at an odd angle, what appeared to be an over-sized cauliflower with tentacles—Gabe couldn't recall the name of the minion but knew they were used in water combat and had the propensity to die quickly—and a fangless vampire. Only after the vampire did Gabe find what he was looking for.

The rat stood suspended in the vat on its hind legs with a digit missing on its left paw and several broken teeth. A mischief of rats could be effective—even taking down an armored adventurer—but a single rat would only be practical in serving as an alarm. He took the tag in his hand and turned it over. The first date had not yet passed. *Twenty-two gold marks for a rat.* He let the tag drop from his hand and sat back on his haunches, putting his face in his hands. There was nothing to do. His energy core was slated to be picked up this evening, which meant by guild law, he had to power his dungeon by midnight. Another postponement would mean a hefty fine and more days without work. He had run out of time and money.

Gabe stood up slowly and dusted off his clothes. He walked back down the row of minions. Eighteen gold marks for the vampire, fifteen for the tentacled cauliflower, twelve for the zombie, and six for the skeleton. The zombie and skeleton had been in the shop for a few months. He could afford the skeleton. That was it. A picture came to his mind; one of him pushing a paper-mache monster on wheels down the hall with a half-skeleton draped over him while a clan stood on the other side laughing and heckling him.

"Sara," he called out.

Moments later, the banshee floated into the room with the

orb in her palm. Gabe had not noticed, but the sparkling light drops were fading and winking out, causing the space to grow dim. *How long have I been here?*

The possessed orb remedied the failing light by racing about, showering more sparks throughout the room.

"You have made your decision, Master Gabe?"

"I will take the minion occupying your first vat," he said, pointing to the partial skeleton.

The orb moved across the room to the first vat, then did a half-turn, pulsing several times.

"The half-skeleton's name is Clack, and it suffers from an unspecified bone disease. What else will you require?"

"Wait. What? Bone disease? Will the minion heal quickly or continually draw down my energy reserves?"

Sara turned to the orb and made a series of gestures before responding. "Aiden says the skeleton should heal after a few weeks. It will draw roughly 120% more energy than normal during that time."

Gabe hoped he lived long enough for energy to be a problem. He could take the hit. "The skeleton will suffice," he said.

"Master Gabe, if I may be so bold," Sara continued when Gabe did not object, "you said you needed minions to defend your dungeon, did you not? Clack will not meet your stated needs."

"I am aware of that," Gabe said. "I...ah... need a hand in the lab. Someone to give me ingredients while I'm mixing on the bench. The skeleton will do nicely until I find a human assistant."

The orb arched over Gabe, showering him with blue sparks. Several landed on his hand and burned. He jumped to one side. "What the hell is going on!" he said, his gaze shifting between the orb and Sara. "I will be taking this up with the store master."

Sara looked surprised, her black eyes darting around the room. She raised her hand, palm up. "Return to me. Return to me."

The sphere zigzagged through space faster than Gabe could follow and settled in Sara's hand.

"What is wrong with it?" Gabe asked.

"Aiden tells me you lie about your needs and are desperate."

Gabe could feel his anger burning. He did not need this. To be called out by minions.

"He also says you smell of sadness. You have lost someone close. He is sorry for you."

Gabe felt hot tears coming down his cheeks and wiped them away with his handkerchief. "I do not need your advice or pity," he said. "You are not humans."

Sara shook her head, "Aiden did not mean to offend." Sara hesitated momentarily, unsure of continuing, "He can sense emotional states. He says you suffer greatly." The orb pulsed vibrantly in her hand. She gasped and mumbled.

"What did it...Aiden...what did Aiden say to you just then?"

He had never seen a minion look uncomfortable, but it was clear from Sara's head movements back and forth that she wanted to be anywhere but in front of him.

"He says the Great Game will crush you and recommends you find another occupation."

Gabe snorted twice, then burst into laughter.

Sara stood still before him, silent, her hair dancing back and forth in the air with the orb vibrating in her palm.

"You sound like my guild advisor," Gabe finally said, having regained his composure. "Not to mention the dungeon builders, my classmates, and me."

"Aiden would like to know why you do it?"

Gabe suddenly realized he was using a banshee to communicate with an orb. *This should feel weirder than it does.* "I don't understand. Are you trying to talk me out of buying this diseased half-skeleton?"

"On the contrary, Aiden thinks he might be able to help. He seems invested in giving you a fighting chance. I do not know why."

Gabe stood silent, mulling over how much he could trust two minions in a consignment store. "The Empress has offered to sponsor new dungeon masters by covering half the cost of the energy cores. That, along with the equipment and savings from my parents, has given me just enough resources to start my dungeon. This is all the opportunity I have for my sick sister and me."

"And what of your work experience?"

"I have some from the lab classes I took. I went to Darkham University and studied at the Apothecary College."

Sara frowned. Even Aiden the orb seemed to dim a bit. "He wants you to succeed, Master Gabe. If he wants that for you," she said, caressing the orb in her hand, "then I want that for you. Heed his warning. The skeleton will not suffice."

"I...I can't afford more." His face burned with shame. He dropped his head and stared intently at the ground. He pulled the coin from his pocket and shrugged his shoulders. "My dungeon is to be powered this very night. If I put it off, I won't have enough money. Only this skeleton..." He trailed off. He felt tears welling up again.

The orb began pulsing again and bounced between Sara's hands.

"Aiden wishes to know about the ring you carry on your right hand."

Gabe splayed his hand out. The emerald gleamed, fixed in place by four golden prongs. The orb drew close to Gabe's hand and rotated over the ring.

"It is not for sale."

"You do not have to sell it. You may pawn the ring for one-quarter of its value and repurchase it within six months if you have the funds. Aiden suggests you purchase Clack, Zet, and Moffet."

"Who are Zet and Moffet?" Gabe asked.

"Zet is the zombie. Moffet is the rat."

"That doesn't seem like much."

The orb jumped up once again and raced around the room.

"Aiden says you will not find a better deal."

Gabe walked over to the vats containing Zet and Moffet and quickly did the math in his head. Forty-four gold marks for the three minions, including transportation. "How much is the ring worth?" He asked as he walked back to the minions.

"Aiden values the ring at 200 gold marks, which means you can pawn it for 50. We will supply the brain pellets and salves you'll need for the minions with the remaining gold. Come back anytime within six months with 60 gold marks to repurchase it."

Gabe sighed. A twenty percent markup to buy his ring back was steep, and he had forgotten that the zombie and rat would require food. "Why the salves?"

"They will help slow the skeleton's bone disease, decrease the zombie's knee pain, and help with the rat's skin problems until your energy core heals them."

"This is ridiculous. I could sell the ring and purchase one of the creatures three or four rows down! Or better yet, hire a summoner and get a couple of high-quality minions without these defects."

"There are reasons why these particular minions are for sale. Whether a curse, injury, or defect, these reasons can be opportunities. Aiden cannot explain why, but he says these three minions are your best opportunity. Also, you are not selling your ring but pawning it. You can repurchase it within six months. Aiden says the odds are against you in all ways, and you will probably die. This is your best chance at succeeding and getting your ring back."

Gabe looked at the orb. "With so much confidence, how can I say no?"

Sara remained quiet and still. It appeared sarcasm was lost on the banshee. He added that to the list of their weaknesses.

"I'll take the creatures," Gabe said finally.

"A wise choice, Master Gabe." The orb pulsed vibrantly in front of her. "Aiden reminds me that Zet, the zombie, has an unidentified curse. It may cause sporadic energy draws."

"Wait, the zombie has a bad leg and is cursed?"

"That is correct. Aiden still believes it to be your best option."

Gabe hesitated and then pulled the ring off his finger. "Let's make this trade before I change my mind."

CHAPTER THREE

Standing on the docks with his arms crossed, Kol'val fiddled with the stoneware beads wrapped around his ponytail, beads Talia had carved as a gift for him on their wedding day. He was dumbfounded. Their goods were being withheld. The Mahajeen was not well and wanted him to go to the city palace to discuss their trade contract, which had stood unchanged for generations. He stared at the envoy, Jaya, whose lithe, ebony figure towered over him. The envoy's lips were moving, but Kol'val wasn't listening.

Do not enter the city. The precept played in his head over and over. It had been one of the first lessons he had learned as a child. He looked to the men of his village unloading the cargo from the boat. Everything around him seemed to speed up at once. Straightening his back to reach his full height, he pulled his hand from his ponytail.

"Why did the Mahajeen not send a surrogate negotiator?" Kol'val asked.

"The information my lord means to give you must be relayed in person. It is highly sensitive," Jaya replied.

Kol'val shook his head. "He knows it is forbidden for us to pass through the city."

"The Mahajeen is appointed by the royal family and is head of commerce for all of Bahavar. He is well aware of the contract and highly values the relationship between our people. I will guide you there myself. You will be safe in my presence."

Kol'val sneered at the insinuation. He was the master trader of Arutua and could defend himself. He also knew damn well who the Mahajeen was and who had appointed him. The Mahajeen would have never asked this of him if he truly understood the relationship between their people. Kol'val glanced over at his men working to unload the cargo, then turned and shifted his gaze past Jaya and up to the golden dome of the palace peeking up above the heart of Bahavar. His mouth was dry, and he found it difficult to swallow.

What does the Mahajeen need to tell me that is so important? To risk everything we have built together? Kol'val thought of the Dai'akan and the Elder council, of seeing the disappointment in their eyes, the sense of betrayal. Would they pronounce death or banishment, or would Pa'vil devour his soul and send him to the underworld to dance with Rua for an eternity?

A glimmer of light appeared in the distance, a thought so simple that he had dismissed it; there was no reason he couldn't come back when the Mahajeen was better or had been replaced.

"Please send my best wishes to the Mahajeen for a speedy recovery. I hope he can meet with me here at the docks in the future." He turned away from Jaya. "Halt," Kol'val yelled. His men stopped in their tracks, looking at him in confusion.

Jaya gripped his arm. "The Mahajeen is dying," he whispered. "If you leave now, the new Mahajeen will know of this insult and void your contract. There will be no trade today or ever. Your boats will not be welcomed back to the city and will be attacked on sight."

Kol'val felt his stomach lurch. "He would do that? For hundreds of years, our people have traded in peace. We are prosperous *together*. Would he throw all of that away? I do not understand."

"You will understand when you speak with him. I assure you, the Mahajeen has his reasons."

Kol'val weighed his options. Gone would be the valuable technology Bahavar supplied; metal tools used to build and maintain the buildings of their village and vast irrigation system, bolts of silk for much of their clothing, spices for their food, and rods and harpoons for fishing. *Talia, would you still love me if I condemn our unborn child to the old ways of bone, sinew, stone, and wood?* He thought of the stories he'd been told, tales of a time before they traded with Bahavar when villagers worked long hours in the fields, struggling to support their children and elders. *How long before everything they built disappeared, and they returned to the old ways? How many would have to die?* His vision blurred. He could not condemn his family and people to that future. His life was a small price to pay.

"Release my arm," Kol'val said.

Jaya obliged and muttered an apology. He took a step back.

"How long will this take?" Kol'val asked.

"No more than a few hours. I have already sent a runner to inform him. Your people are his priority, and he will clear his schedule to meet with you. When done, the Mahajeen will send a runner, and your goods will be released."

Kol'val looked at the blazing circle sitting on the horizon.

Pa'vil guide and protect me. Forgive me if you can.

He turned to his men, "Continue unloading the cargo," he said. "I will go with Jaya. Under no circumstances are you to follow me."

"You cannot...." Tamar, his first in command, said. Others echoed Tamar's concern.

"I can and I will," Kol'val declared, "Pa'vil willing." His men appeared startled by his defiant tone and invocation of Pa'vil's name. They grew silent. "Jaya, will lead the way. If I am not back by the time the sun peaks in the sky, load the cargo and go home without me."

Kol'val shifted his weight and squared himself towards Jaya, "I will follow." He did not look back. He wanted to. He wanted to explain his reasoning but did not want to show weakness.

At the end of the wood slats that made up the docks, Kol'val hesitated with his foot hovering over the packed dirt. A fishmonger was setting up across the street while two fat men who looked like kin quarreled while steering a horse-cart past him. Kol'val gave the horse a sideways glance. He had never seen one so close. He took another step. Nothing happened. He looked around and then down at his feet, mildly surprised. Pa'vil had not struck him down. He glanced down the street at Jaya, who was watching him with arms folded. Kol'val asked Pa'vil, Talia, and his unborn child for forgiveness, then took another step.

He went through the city with buildings looming over him like noisy beasts, foreign and suffocating. He thought of the wonder he had held for Bahavar standing on the dock for the first time as a young man. On approach, the city had looked like something out of a dream; the heat shimmers had caused the sky and surrounding dunes to dance and bleed with the creams and whites and golds of the buildings. Deep in his heart, he had wanted to explore the city and feared he would enjoy the journey.

Jaya turned abruptly down an alley. Kol'val followed and tried to keep from gagging as the stench of sweat and sewage mixed with the pungent aroma of meats and fruit. More and more people appeared in the windows and out in the streets. A child clipped him in the side as he ran by, chased by a girl shaking her fists. Kol'val attracted glances but was mostly ignored.

The Ghabi Bazaar, as Jaya called it, was the worst of it. Rows of merchants shouted and gesticulated at Kol'val on either side, hawking their wares; sweetmeat stalls, barrels of spices and dyes, seeds, nuts and fruits, glittering jewelry, ornate rugs, and clay pots stacked high, all vied for his attention. He yelled over the clamor to Jaya, asking if a less occupied route existed to the royal palace. Jaya turned towards Kol'val, his face taking on a grave expression, "Any other route would keep the Mahajeen waiting." They continued, and as they exited the Bazaar onto a wide street, Jaya stopped and gestured. With all the distractions, Kol'val had not noticed how close they were to the palace. It was the largest building Kol'val had ever seen, stretching an entire city block, with glistening white pillars as thick as the oldest trees of Arutua marching around its periphery. Jaya led him to the front of the building, where a set of steps led to an archway flanked by two winged creatures. Four men stood at the entrance, dressed in pale green uniforms with scimitars strapped to their backs. One of them, with three red stripes on his lapel, gave Kol'val a cursory glance before nodding to Jaya, then returned to his conversation with the other guardsmen.

Inside, frescos of humans on beasts of burden battling creatures covered the vaulted ceilings, and finely-woven tapestries draped the walls. There were sculptures with faces so detailed that Kol'val felt the hairs on his neck stand up when he looked at them. The floor was smooth and complex, with a dizzying mixture of white and brown swirls interspersed with flecks of red and gold. Kol'val was keenly aware of his sandals slapping against the floor.

Jaya led him through a door, then a series of hallways that emptied into a foyer.

"I will announce you to the Mahajeen. Please, have a seat." Jaya motioned to a nearby chair.

Kol'val walked over and sat down. He realized he was facing a wall with a painting of the Mahajeen himself, looking up from his desk with a quill in one hand and the other lying flat on a stack of parchment. The artist captured the Mahajeen's appearance; his corpulent figure, sparse gray hair, ruddy complexion, and bulbous nose. It was not flattering, but it was accurate. Kol'val then looked down the foyer and noted that the other paintings were of his predecessors in a similar pose. Kol'val had met with many of them during his time as the master trader.

"The Mahajeen will see you," Jaya announced and opened a door.

Kol'val got up with his teeth clenched and his hands balled into fists. The route here had been full of wonders and distractions, but looking at the various Mahajeens across time reminded him of his duty.

He was greeted with the strong smell of tobacco. The room was dimly lit with a rug of black and red swirls running between the entrance and the Mahajeen's desk.

The anger left Kol'val when he saw the Mahajeen lying back in his chair. His skin sagged off his bones, and his breathing appeared labored.

"It is not the first time I have seen such a reaction, my friend," the Mahajeen said. He launched into a series of coughs and brought a handkerchief to dab at his mouth.

"It is true. You do not look well." Kol'val said.

The Mahajeen laughed. "Never one for subtlety, Kol'val.

Please..." He motioned for Kol'val to sit in a chair before his desk. "I see Jaya was able to convince you to come. I must be honest, Kol'val, I did not think you would, but I am glad you did."

"I almost didn't. When I informed Jaya of my intention to return later, he threatened to nullify the contract and attack our boats on sight!"

Jaya walked in carrying a tray of water and fruits and offered them. Kol'val declined with a shake of his head while the Mahajeen drank deeply from a cup and placed it on his desk. Jaya bowed and left.

"You are owed an explanation."

Kol'val was not sure what to say. What could be worth betraying his god and his people? He gazed into the Mahajeen's haunted eyes, a look he had seen only in the Dai'akan after a pilgrimage. It spoke of anguish he couldn't quite grasp. Maybe that's why he felt uncomfortable. He remained quiet.

"There is harmony between our people. I know what I have asked of you and appreciate your trust." The Mahajeen glanced past Kol'val to the doorway and back to him, licking his lips. "We are in a war, Kol'val," the Mahajeen's voice dropped to a whisper, "and we are losing. Badly. Empress Inalda's line is advancing and ravaging our numbers by the day. I do not know how much longer we can hold out."

Bad news, indeed, Kol'val thought. The Mahajeen had the weight of his people on his shoulders. Arutua would have to return to the old ways unless they could find a new trading partner. "I am sorry, but your war does not concern me."

"If I thought that, I would have had a surrogate warn you, make the trade, then wave goodbye, knowing that your people were safe and mine were doomed. But that is not the case."

"What do you mean?"

"My sources tell me one of her main suppliers has been destroyed."

"Supplier of what?"

"Dark magic; potions, enhancers, bombs, weapons that give her army a keen advantage. She has issued an edict to recruit more soldiers and bolster her numbers while she searches for new suppliers."

"This does not involve my people."

"Not yet. The Empress has mouths to feed. The Mage Guild and the Great Game operate on otai. She has harvested almost every drop within her kingdom and pushes into our territories to secure more before her stores are depleted."

Kol'val thought of the otai the Dai'akan would bring down from Mount Laiya. He did not like where this was going.

"Do you think my people have not noticed?" the Mahajeen continued, "In trades long past, you were my elder, and now you look to be but a young man while I stand at my grave—the items you bring for trade: pots, baskets, flutes, and drums, are practically indestructible and last generations. The Empress and mages hunt for your island. They will find you," the Mahajeen leaned forward, "and when they do, it will be your war to fight."

Kol'val leaned forward in his chair, staring down the Mahajeen. "How do I know you are not working for her?"

The Mahajeen laughed, interlacing his hands across his stomach as if he were a fat man again. "No, my friend, if I were a villain, you and your men would be dead, tortured until we got every last drop of information from you."

It felt as if a great weight were placed on Kol'val's chest. He struggled even to catch his breath. He had just been angry, but he could not pinpoint what he felt anymore, just an undefined dread. This Empress Inalda and her mages threatened everything he knew, yet what were they compared to Pa'vil?

The Mahajeen reached over one side of his chair and brought up a large wooden box covered with intricate carvings of animals. "I cannot offer much, but I can offer this. A tooth to give you more power in your bite." He opened the box with a click and spun it around. Kol'val stood up as the Mahajeen lifted the lid. He could not believe his eyes. Inside the box was the Dai'akan's soul dagger pulsing green in the dim light. "I see from the look on your face that you recognize the rarity of this object. The mages are powerful, their bodies hardened from prolonged use of otai, but this dagger will cut through their skin and kill them."

With a lick of his lips, Kol'val leaned forward to inspect the dagger. A pale green bulb pulsed below the translucent ivory handle. The long, thin blade was double-edged with a ridge running up the center. It was an exact match. Whispers spoke of the dagger and staff being forged by Pa'vil himself before the Seeding. *Could he have made more than one? The blade is divine and belongs to Pa'vil.* The possibility of two Dai'akans existing, sharing the responsibility of guiding the people and serving Pa'vil, intrigued Kol'val. When the enemy came for them, Kol'val could stand with Masima and fight, soul daggers in hand. He felt a warmth in his chest spread out to his fingertips. *But why help us?* A seed of doubt remained.

"We did not trade for it. What do you want?" Kol'val asked.

"A stronger partner," the Mahajeen replied. "The Empress will come for your otai, Kol'val. And when she does, you will fight back with this." He gestured to the dagger.

Kol'val stood still, eyeing the blade like a viper ready to strike. Finally, he grabbed the hilt, pulling the dagger from its resting place. The cold ivory felt good against his palm.

After Kol'val left, the Mahajeen slumped heavily against his desk. *Wrap the lie in a blanket of truth, and it will sell. The Mage had been right.* Part of him wanted Kol'val to laugh, spit in his face, and walk out. But Kol'val had been seduced by that dagger, a thing of black magic forged in the fires of the Magi, the Mahajeen was sure. The price was high, but so be it if it cemented his family's future; a title and land for his eldest and a stipend so that his wife and remaining children could live comfortably. The Mahajeen sneered at his thoughts, "As if I had a choice?" he mumbled. He was so tired. *Death cannot come soon enough.*

CHAPTER FOUR

"You did what?" Miranda stood up and braced herself with one hand on the desk. A weak light hit the side of her face from the apartment window, accentuating her ashen complexion. Her black hair was pulled back into a bun, making her expression more severe.

"The ring is mine, just as that locket is yours," he gestured to Miranda. "If there had been another way, I would've taken it."

She grasped the pendant around her neck, squeezed it tightly with her free hand, and released it. "I'm not accusing you, Gabe. I worry that you won't be able to get it back, is all." She tipped her head down slightly and coughed.

"Try to stay calm, Miranda. I don't want you to get into a coughing fit. Don't worry. I'll get the ring back. Now that I have adequate protection, I can focus on making money. You should see them, Miranda. They are fierce creatures."

"Three minions are a lot better than one. I'm just sorry you had to pawn your ring. It means so very much to you."

"I said I will get it back, and I mean it."

"I have no doubt," Miranda said with an encouraging smile. "Will you stay and have tea and biscuits with me? Colin Burke will be by to visit shortly."

Gabe tried to keep the disdain from his voice. "I will pass. I have much to do. The energy core awaits pickup."

She tapped the desk with her finger as she studied Gabe's face. "I should not have mentioned Colin."

"Why?"

"Gabe, you need to work on your poker face. I can understand your dislike for him, but he has been kind to me, more so during my sickness. And he visits even when my so-called 'friends' do not. I admit his conversation is sometimes skewed, but I enjoy his company. I like how he looks at me."

"You enjoy company, and company enjoys you. Just be careful, or you'll have a proposal before long."

"Am I leading him on by accepting his company?"

Gabe shrugged. "Leading him on or not, Colin has always looked at you that way. I had to stomach his puppy-love look all through school. He doesn't have the nerve to ask for your hand. In the meantime, he will busy himself to be near you at every opportunity."

"Perhaps I would accept a proposal if I could be sure I would live long enough to see the wedding," Miranda said. "There is warmth in having a companion."

Gabe took a step towards his sister and kneeled. "He doesn't deserve you, Miranda. I will make enough to buy a cure or find one, and then you can choose whomever you wish."

Miranda reached out and grasped his hand. "Do be careful. Dungeon-mastering is a dangerous business. One whisper to the wrong person, and you could lose everything. I would lose everything. I don't think I could bear it, not after..." She searched Gabe's face.

They hugged, then Gabe quickly pulled away and started to

talk in a jumble. "It took months to get to the point where I could think about something other than mother and father. Curing your illness and getting this dungeon up and running carried me. They are all I think about, Miranda. I've been scrambling up this mountain for so long that I don't even know what I'm doing half the time. But this morning, when I got those minions, I felt like I could stop, take a breath, and look around. And you know what? I liked what I saw. We're doing this."

Miranda wiped a tear from her cheeks and laughed. She touched Gabe's face. "Okay," she said with a firm nod, "together, we can do this."

A knock on the door caused Gabe to jump to his feet. He wiped at his face with his hand and waited for Miranda to take a seat so she could receive company. When he opened the door, Colin took a step back. With slicked-back dark hair and a white-toothed smile, he looked like a traveling salesman.

"Gabe? Good to see you, ol' buddy. Is Miranda there? Oh, there you are," he said with a wave. "We have a standing engagement these days. I cannot get enough of her conversation. She has excellent advice on all practical matters."

Before Gabe could respond, Miranda said, "Stop making me blush. Do come in, Colin."

Gabe pulled the door back and made a sweeping gesture. Colin took a few steps into the room, twirled, then went down on bended knee and took Miranda's hand in his own.

"Always the gentleman, Colin. Welcome." She looked past Colin to see Gabe's grimace.

"Gabe, will you be joining us? I'd love to hear about your preparations for your dungeon," Colin said, standing back up and turning towards him.

"He will not be staying, unfortunately. He has important errands to run," Miranda said.

47

"Yes, I'm afraid my dungeon is nearing completion, and I must make a few more trips before the day's out."

Colin looked surprised. "Nearing completion, you say? Why Gabe, that is excellent news. You've been talking about it for so long."

"I just purchased three minions."

"That's a good start. We just got attacked not two weeks past by a clan. I've been too busy making potions to see the memory crystal. With the Empress sponsoring all these new dungeons, riff-raff are getting in on the Great Game. The guilds are going to make a fortune."

"I could've purchased more, mind you, but my minions are strong enough and will do for now," Gabe said.

"You didn't tell me you were attacked, Colin. How did it go?" Miranda asked, glaring at Gabe.

"I didn't think it was worth mentioning until now, honestly. They were slaughtered to the very last soul. It was a messy business, but it couldn't be helped. Any survivors could go back and report our location. Our dungeon is large—likely not large enough to appeal to the high-tiered adventurers— but one never knows. Best not to tempt fate and all that." Colin stopped talking suddenly and looked back and forth at Miranda and Gabe. "I'm not implying that Aatma or your parents did anything wrong. That shocked us all. A great tragedy, please...."

"No offense taken, Colin," Miranda said calmly with a raised hand. "You cannot control everything." She looked at Gabe, who kept his eyes locked on Colin.

"Especially when you are just a lab worker," Gabe added.

"Good points all around," Colin chuckled nervously. "I hope to have enough money to start a proper dungeon one day. In the meantime, I'll get plenty of experience." Colin looked down at the ground and tapped his foot briefly before continuing, "When do you think you'll be ready to open the dungeon? No, no, don't tell me. After all, we will be competitors. Friendly, I hope, like a big brother and little brother in a wrestling match. You'll get there with a bit of hard work and luck."

"I will get there," Gabe said, "tell me, Apothecary Burke, what potions do they have you working on this week?"

Colin glanced over at Miranda. She returned his look with a weak smile. "The disfigurement potion, you mean? Very tricky to get just right. It takes a steady hand."

"Oh?" Gabe said, ignoring the deepening scowl on Miranda's face.

Colin shifted from side to side.

Miranda stood up. "I will remind Gabe of his pending responsibilities and not have him overstay out of mere politeness. You and I have much to discuss, Colin. You can tell me all about your work. No trade secrets, of course." She walked past Colin and Gabe to the entrance. "Brother, I will talk with you again soon. Please, be careful."

"I will try, dear sister." Gabe kissed her on the cheek and bowed slightly towards Colin. "If you'll excuse me."

GABE STEPPED out into the warm evening air and weaved through the crowded streets, past the five city blocks housing the famed flower markets and the central square. When he rounded onto the red-brick mansions of Guild Row with the city walls looming behind them, his mind veered towards his upcoming meeting with Master Ezil, the gatekeeper for energy cores in the district, who had a reputation for being temperamental.

He signed in at the front desk and was escorted past the smoke-filled lounge to the offices upstairs. The hall was carpeted in a deep red, and the polished wood lining the walls shone in the glow of candlelight. His escort stopped towards the end of the hallway and knocked on a plain wooden door, announcing Dungeon Master Gabriel Shook. When Ezil bade him enter to sit, the escort shut the door behind Gabe. He listened to the man's soft footsteps retreat while Ezil scribbled on parchment at his desk. Ezil motioned for him to sit, and Gabe complied. He was about to say something when Ezil raised a finger and continued writing with his other hand.

"You have been practicing the joining ceremony?" Ezil finally asked, dropping the ink pen. He raised and tilted his head slightly backward, peering down at Gabe with eyes made large by thick spectacles. "The council was split on its decision to grant you a core. I voted 'nay.'"

"I see," Gabe shifted in his seat. The room suddenly seemed small.

"I tell you this not out of admonishment but out of respect for your parents. The Empress's largesse has lifted many fools into the Great Game. I did not want you to be one of them.

Gabe nodded, then mumbled his thanks to the Empress. *Did he insult me?* He felt sweat trickling down his temple.

"I'm not looking for platitudes, boy." Ezil sighed. "Mark my words. A quick death awaits you. Your parents could have started a dungeon. They had a passion and understanding for potion-making and could have gone far. But they tempered their ambition. They survived and prospered under Aatma's guidance."

"Look where that got them."

"Yes, look! A family. You and your sister are grown and educated with bright futures."

"My parents are gone, Master Ezil, and my sister is sick with consumption. I do not seek glory. I do not seek riches. I want my sister to live. I want her to have the bright future my parents paid for with their lives," he said the last part in a whisper, but his tone was defiant, and Ezil looked away first.

"I'm sorry," Ezil said with a heavy sigh. He opened the drawer in his desk, pulled out a plain wooden box, and opened it. Inside lay gloves, tongs, and a milky white cube with blood-red lines undulating across its surface. A pungent odor, like bleach, permeated the air. "All of your paperwork is in order." Ezil closed the lid and pushed the box across the desk. "Try not to kill yourself."

CHAPTER FIVE

"No killing. No raping. No pillaging," Captain Ian Ryall said, pacing back and forth on the deck of the Stork. Except for the slight fading of his blue uniform, he appeared to be the model of discipline, with a freshly-shaven face and salt and pepper hair cut short. His men stood in a line at attention.

"We are here to capture and transport." He stopped and turned abruptly, "Beetle, did you hear that?"

Beetle's smile showed a mixture of brown and yellow teeth. His thick chest hair stuck out of his shirt, and his pants hung loosely on his thick frame.

"Aye, Sir, no killing, raping, or pillaging." Beetle held a smile and squinted, looking over at the Captain. "A question then, sir?"

"Is it serious, or are you taking the piss out of me?"

"A bit of both, sir."

The men laughed.

It was the first time since picking up the mages that Beetle had heard laughter. For all of Captain Ryall's pomp and ceremony, the man had a firm grasp on the ship's morale and knew a little banter could go a long way in relieving tension.

As the first rank, Beetle was used to playing the part. How he'd managed to get his position was a mystery to him. *If you survive long enough, you're bound to be promoted.* For whatever reason, the men respected his banter with the Captain.

"Don't make me regret this, Beetle. Permission granted."

"What's the bloody point if we can't have some fun?" Beetle asked.

Another laugh.

"Careful," Captain Ryall said, wagging his finger back and forth. "You are on the edge of insubordination."

"No offense meant, sir. We leave the comfort of our homes and stick our necks out. And for what?"

"For honor," Captain Ryall said.

"For gold," yelled the men in unison.

"That too," Captain Ryall replied, the corners of his mouth twitching, fighting a smile.

The men stayed at attention, but Beetle could feel them relaxing.

"As good a reason as any, I guess," he said with a shrug.

The moment the offer to re-up was made, Beetle, who had been mildly drunk then, signed on the dotted line. He had been swabbing decks, hauling food from the kitchen, and scrambling up the rigging since he was a boy. It was all he knew, and he knew it well.

"Anyone else have a question?" Captain Ryall asked.

Leonid, a lanky, freckled lad barely out of puberty with hair as red as copper, spoke up. "Why aren't they using their ships? And why won't they tell us where we're going?"

There were a few nods and grunts in the line.

There it is, Beetle thought. *The men had gained enough confidence to ask the right questions. Brave boy, that Leonid.*

"The mages are in a hurry," Captain Ryall said. "I will let them speak for themselves shortly, but my order is clear. If you need to defend yourself, so be it, but know that there will be a reward for every person captured unharmed. If you disobey my orders, you will answer to the mages."

The men cogitated on his words while water lapping against the hull filled the silence. Captain Ryall was about to speak when a creaking was heard from the stairs below deck. The men swiveled their heads in unison, and a small figure appeared covered in thick robes. Beetle was disappointed when the figure reached up and pulled back the hood, revealing an ordinary-looking man in his middle years with spectacles and a goatee.

"Good day," he said with a heavy accent, overpronouncing each word with his hands crossed before him. "I am Elendr, emissary to the mages. Captain, if I may?"

Captain Ryall gave a curt nod and stepped to the side of the line at attention.

Elendr approached the men. "I heard your questions," he said, gesturing towards Leonid. "You ask yourselves why the Mage Guild enlists you in such a mission as this?"

The emissary walked down the line, eyeing each person in turn. Beetle felt his muscles tense when Elendr looked at him. *Can they read our minds?*

"Something was taken from us long ago. We want it back. Simple. We are grateful for your help in recollecting what was lost, and you will be rewarded handsomely for your troubles."

There was a moment of silence, ostensibly to see if there were any questions. Beetle had a hundred of them, as did the others, he was sure, but he did not know this man's temperament and thought it best to direct further inquiries to the Captain in private.

"A mage prepares to guide us," Elendr hesitated momentarily, rubbing his goatee with his thumb and forefinger. "He will be up on the deck in his own time. It is important that he not be disturbed. Understood?"

The men remained silent.

Captain Ryall repeated the question sharply, "Is that understood?"

"Yes, sir," came the reply in unison.

Beetle's heart quickened when Elendr pulled his hood back over his head and returned below deck without another word. Stories had been whispered between the crew when the mages had boarded in the night, horror stories of people falling on the wrong side of the guild and being found flayed or dismembered or any number of grotesque scenarios. Usually, stories that varied were nonsense, but they *could be* true.

After spending the day tarring the standing rigging, the night saw Beetle fast asleep on the deck wrapped in a blanket, a benefit of the warm air this time of year, when Leonid's shouts woke him from his slumber. He looked about in confusion and saw Leonid with a torch next to the mainmast looking up and trembling. It took a moment for Beetle's vision to sharpen, but when it did, he saw a figure shimmying up the mainmast with the frenetic speed of an insect.

Leonid started to yell again but then abruptly stopped. He looked around, his face crimson, and bent down to pick up what looked like a cowl. Beetle jumped to his feet and padded across the deck.

"Who is that?" he commanded, pointing to the figure.

"I w-was patrolling port-side," Leonid stammered, "when I heard a noise. I saw glowing eyes, Beetle. So fast. I've never...," his voice faltered. "Elendr should have warned us. Who climbs the mainmast naked in the middle of the night?" Leonid asked.

Beetle took the torch. "Easy, boy, a bloody mage is who. Well, you knew enough to shut your mouth instead of carrying on hollerin', eh?" He backed away from the mast holding the torch high. The light barely reached the bottom of the crow's nest.

"I think he's pointing out to sea," Leonid said. He cocked his head and listened. "Sounds like he's laughing."

Peering up at the shadows dancing on the mast, Beetle heard the high-pitched cackle. *Just what we need, a mage who has lost his wits. Is there any other kind?* "Your vision is better than mine," Beetle said. "Our instructions were straightforward enough. He's giving us a direction. Inform Soko to change course to wherever that mage is pointing."

Leonid frowned. He was still shaking badly.

Beetle slapped him across the face and put a finger up.

"Follow my orders, boy, or we'll both be answering to the mages. If you don't mind," Beetle returned the torch to him, "I'm going back to sleep."

Beetle tossed and turned as that incessant cackling drifted down from above. Finally, he resigned himself to staying up. He stared out into the darkness and wondered how he had ended up on a ship being led by a madman. *The Captain must have been in some serious trouble to take this assignment.*

Ian sat in a high-backed chair with his lunch, boiled salt-beef stew, and biscuits with a pudding bowl off to one side. He read a list of his debts, a painful reminder of why he had a cargo hold full of mages. No one else in the city was willing to take them on, but he had been bought. He dunked the biscuit into the stew and took a bite. *Soras is a master of harvesting flavor from the most meager of ingredients.*

Ian had managed to keep his shipping business afloat after his business partner had absconded from the city with the magistrate's wife and a sizeable portion of the company funds. On the brink of bankruptcy, with an estate and business leveraged to the hilt, the honorable Captain Ryall had been weeks away from debtor's prison. He had resigned himself to his fate, letting the Stork sit in the dock unused, when a broker had approached him with an offer: transport the mages to an island to recover stolen property, bring back the offenders, and all of his debts would be paid in advance with a promise of more when the mission was complete. Success or not, the Mage Guild would pay his debts in full.

His wife, Meera, had disapproved. She knew well the stories of the mages, a variant of what was whispered in secret between the men on his ship, of treachery and death for those who entered into a contract with them. She was adamant that her family could loan them money. That proposal had cemented his decision to take the contract. He would rather be in debtor's prison than take her family's money.

A knock came from the door jolting Ian from his thoughts.

"Enter," he said, turning the paper over and leaving it on his desk.

Elendr walked in, pulling his hood back. "I did not know you were eating, Captain. I can come back."

"No, please. Come, sit down. I was finishing," he said.

The emissary approached the desk. "You have hardly touched your lunch, Captain. You are sure?"

Ian waved a dismissive hand. "Stay, please. My appetite is not what it should be these days. I am glad you are here, Elendr. The mage up in the crow's nest has spooked my men."

"Yes, I could not foresee when he would appear. My apologies, Captain."

Ian stretched and then interlaced his hands, resting them on the desk. He sat forward and met Elendr's eyes. "Once, when I was a boy, my father took me to a public hanging. The platform held five people at a time. One was a man covered in filth. He fought and spit, but he went slack when they put the rope around his neck and looked right at me. I was in a crowd of hundreds of people packed together, but he looked at me like I am with you. Then he tilted his head back and cried piteously. A few moments later, he was dead. There was a madness in his eyes that I had not seen again until this morning."

"An interesting tale, Captain, but I assure you he guides us true if that is your concern."

"He is visible to all on my deck, Elendr. His condition cannot be ignored."

"There is a strain on you and your men. I see that, Captain. But the mage you call mad makes this mission possible and gives you and your men the opportunity for a handsome recompense. If he makes your men uncomfortable, then you quell their fears. Your men serve because they trust you, Captain, and want to get paid. Do your job, and we will do ours."

Ian shifted at his desk. He was not used to being ordered around on his ship. "Okay."

"Good." Elendr rubbed his goatee and smiled.

"We have a direction now. Of that, I am thankful. Do you have any idea when we will arrive? A timeframe I can relay to my men?"

"I do not, but there is a chance we will not see our destination when we arrive."

"I don't understand," Ian said.

"Our destination is most likely veiled. Nothing dangerous," Elendr said quickly, holding up his hands, "merely a spell to trick light and remain unseen from passersby."

"And what of the inhabitants? Will they fire on us from behind this veil?"

"No, Captain, my masters will bring down the spell long before we are within firing range. The danger is minimal. As best we can tell, the island's people, a few dozen, are peaceful. The key to success will be to move quickly and confidently."

"And if these 'peaceful guests' decide to revolt on the way back?"

"The way back does not concern us. My masters have ways of calming people and may even choose to harness the wind so we return faster. I see now the question in your eyes, Captain." Elendr smiled before continuing, "Why do we not harness the wind to speed ourselves to the island? I would prefer that, too, but we track another boat and must pace ourselves. So, Captain, you see, there is a method to our 'madness.' Share this information with your crew if you wish, put their hearts at ease."

Ian sat at his desk long after Elendr had left, staring at nothing, thinking through everything he had been told. He remained that way until the cook came for his mostly uneaten lunch. With a furrowed brow and drooping mustache, Soras did not hide his disapproval, but he sensed the Captain's mood and did not comment.

"Soras, bring Beetle to me," he said.

"Yes, Captain," Soras replied, scuttling out of the room.

CHAPTER SIX

The sun sat above the horizon, spraying light through a patchwork of gossamer clouds as Gabe stepped through the western gates. Merchants, guildmembers, soldiers, and peasants alike streamed out on wagons, horseback, and on foot, the last traffic of the day before the gates closed. Gabe eyed the guard near him, whose left ear looked like a dog had chewed on it. He clutched the box containing the energy core close to his body, worried that he might be asked to show its contents, but the guard waved him through with barely a glance. He followed the road several hundred meters to the main fork and continued west into a short grass field, stepping into the shade of a thick canopy of trees. He turned and watched the people on the road from the comfort of the forest. When he was sure no one was watching, he moved deeper into the trees, zigzagging as he went and pausing periodically to listen.

Moonlight bathed the trees in a soft glow when Gabe arrived at his dungeon. The entrance was marked by a pair of basement doors on one side of a small field. A green blanket covered the doors, blending them with the surrounding grass. It was a neat and inexpensive camouflage he had learned from his parents. Gabe wanted to run straight to the dungeon doors and yank them open. He resisted the urge. Instead, he circled the perimeter of the clearing, pausing and watching even as raindrops fell. When he was sure he was alone, he scurried to the entrance from the forest's edge, pulled back the doors, and descended into the vestibule.

Gabe inhaled deeply, taking in the smell of stone and earth. Years of planning and hard work led to this moment. *How long have I spent practicing the joining ritual?* He wished his parents and Miranda could have been here to see the halls and laboratory. They weren't much, but they were his.

To one side, a torch and tinder box sat on a stone shelf at eye level. Gabe sat the energy core on the ground, then pulled out the flint and steel from the tinder box along with dry needles he had collected several days prior. After nurturing a single tendril of smoke into a small flame, Gabe lit a torch dipped in Bayberry wax. He placed the tinderbox back on the stone shelf, snuffed out the fire, then closed the doors to the entrance.

He had settled on a simple design for his dungeon. It was symmetric with the vestibule, a small chamber inside the entrance, splitting into two paths, one to the right and one to the left. The paths extended a few meters before making 90-degree turns and running parallel down long hallways. Those hallways opened up to a room on the opposite end, about twice the size of the vestibule, with a single iron door leading to his laboratory. The builder had told him, "There is elegance in simplicity," but the truth was more practical; it was all he could afford. Gabe ran his hand across the cool stone. *Soon, this all will be covered with dungeon skin.* He went down the hallway with the torch in one hand and the boxed energy core tucked under the other arm.

The lock made a hard click when Gabe turned the key, and the groan of metal scraping against stone echoed down the hallways when he pushed the door. The laboratory was the most expensive part of the dungeon, mainly from the large transport circle taking up a third of the room. Two tables were on his left, flanked by high stools. Beyond them, bookshelves ran the wall length sparsely populated with university textbooks. Just next to the door where Gabe stood was a foldable cot and a pillow, allowing him a place to sleep. Two fume hoods stood at the opposite wall from the entrance, venting into the field above. A well was next to the fume hoods with brick built around it in a circle. The well cost had been a wild card at the outset of the building process, but luck favored Gabe, as the water had been close to the surface. In the far corner of the room, off to his right beyond the transport circle, was a simple hole in the floor used as a toilet and for trash. The energy from the core could burn whatever waste was produced.

Gabe lit several candles on the benches, walked around the transport circle to the far side of the room, and faced a square hole in the wall about the size of his fist. He put the torch in a sconce to one side, opened the box, slipped on the thick leather gloves, and grabbed the pincers. Carefully, he picked up the energy core with the pincers and placed it into the hole in the wall. The light from the vibrant red and white swirls cast swimming patterns across the laboratory's borders. Gabe felt like he was peeking into a vast unknown, and a warmth spread through him. His thoughts wandered to his sister, Miranda, and her sickness, to Master Ezil and his disapprobation, and then to his parents. He felt like he was on a boat, riding those red swirls, waves on an ocean of light.

The fusion incantation sprouted from his lips without thought. As he spoke, the swirls crimsoned and became turbulent, losing some of their forms, beating against an unseen barrier, struggling to break free. Gabe felt emotion in his words, words that had heretofore been without life, merely recited a thousand times. The swirls broke free from their confines and raced across the walls. The air before Gabe grew thick with a red mist. He did not move and continued the incantation even as the world around him disappeared.

Swirls of reds and whites blanketed his vision, syncing with his pulse. A splash of bright red infused the dancing colors, a warm and familiar red—*my blood*. Something was cocooned with him as he floated in those colors. They joined, and his body spasmed. Power coursed through him. A deep sound thrummed in the distance as if the earth had chimed in at their joining.

The colors waned and then vanished from his vision. Gabe slumped to the stone floor like a marionette cut from its strings, drenched in sweat. The leather gloves and pincers were scattered on the ground before him. He glanced up, expecting to see the energy core in the wall, but a thin membrane of what looked to be skin covered the hole. The skin was spreading, crawling across the walls of the dungeon. Just under the skin, bright, pulsing white and red veins shone through. Gabe reached out and touched the glowing membrane and recoiled in shock. He felt the stroke from his finger as if he had touched his skin.

He struggled to stand and cross the room, his muscles feeling like water and his skin burning. The room spun around him. His hip hit a hard edge, and he tipped over and smacked his face against a wooden surface. *A table, I'm on a table.* He reached out and pulled himself forward with his sweaty palms. Glass shattered nearby. Gabe stopped and rolled onto his back.

He saw skin crawl across the ceiling of his laboratory and felt it as his own, then turned his head, vomited, and cried. He closed his eyes and dreamt of flesh and stone.

Gabe's back felt numb, and his body ached when he moved onto his side into the fetal position. He licked his parched lips and grimaced at the taste of bile. With one eye cracked open, he studied his surroundings. *My dungeon.* He reached out in his mind and ran through the laboratory. He felt the weight of his body and table on the floor, the burnt-out torch resting in the sconce, the soft leather of the gloves, even the tinderbox. They all pressed against new parts of him. Birds chirped from somewhere above. He tilted his head and looked at the flutes and their vents disappearing into the ceiling.

A rhythmic prodding pushed against his consciousness, like a forgotten item on the verge of being remembered. He propped himself up on the table and looked around. That sensation was forgotten when he spotted the well and lurched forward. Gabe tied a bucket to the rope and lowered it. He heard a splash, then hauled the water back up. His fingers fumbled twice with the heavier weight, and he cursed and gripped harder each time. When the bucket appeared above the lip of the stone, he pulled it out, placed it on the ground, stuck his head inside, and took big gulps of water.

While sitting against the wall next to the well, Gabe felt a nudge at the edge of his mind again and realized what he was sensing. *The joining is complete. My transport ring is powered.* He stood up slowly and walked to the seven nested concentric circles. Each circle was composed of Haqi symbols etched in a shallow furrow of the stone. The dungeon's skin covered the area, dipping slightly into the furrows. Gabe felt the familiar nudge at the edge of his consciousness each time the rings pulsed a soft white.

He put his hands on the table to support himself and

closed his eyes. The nudge came again, and he let it pass. He felt a gathering of energy and a release of heat. A wall of white light erupted from the outermost ring, traveling up to the ceiling in the blink of an eye. He turned away, shielding his face with his forearm. The bright light dissipated, and the room returned to the soft reds and whites of energy veins emanating from the dungeon walls. In the middle of the transport ring were a bag of brain pellets, three ointment jars, a zombie, half a skeleton, and a rat.

SHE STEPPED through the doors of the consignment store and smiled at the blind banshee named Sara and her orb companion, Aiden. She told them she was interested in buying a minion for her dungeon. They led her through the dusty aisles stacked with junk to a room full of discarded creatures.

"I'm looking for a specific minion," she said, fiddling with the ring on her left hand. When she described the creature, the banshee stated she could not comment on past inventory, given their confidentiality agreement. Sapphire knew arguing was pointless, but she couldn't help showing her disappointment. When the orb zoomed by, she snatched it out of the air. The minion struggled in her hand, but she drew on her power and held it firm. Sara looked panicked as Sapphire squeezed the ball tighter and tighter until it popped in her hand. She looked at Sara, whose face was distorted with grief.

"You're a banshee, aren't you? So, let's hear you scream."

Sara screamed, and Sapphire drew on her power and bathed in their pain.

CHAPTER SEVEN

W hen he spotted the trading boats approaching, a boy with jet-black hair and spindly legs enthusiastically rang the village bell. Ioane didn't bother looking up. She sat on the steps leading up to one of the Elder's huts with thread in hand. Even the constant reminder of her worsening tremor couldn't touch her sanguinity as her mottled hands struggled to put another bead on the bracelet she was making for her goddaughter, Talia.

Palani sat on the step below her, looking at the bell in the distance. "The longing has guided them home true," she said.

Ioane smiled when she slipped the bead successfully onto the thread. "As it always does, praise Pa'vil," Ioane replied. *Kol'val will get to see the birth of his child after all.* "How fares Talia this morning?"

"Nauseous, the bitter ginger brew is helping, but she struggles to eat."

"A good sign, nausea. It means the baby requires much from her and is gaining strength."

"She would not be displeased if the baby came early. She

66

only wanted Kol'val to be here. I should probably go wake her." Palani braced herself to stand up. "She will be eager to see the boats for herself."

"Breathe deeply, Palani. The boats will be a while yet. Let Talia come on her own time."

"Hmm," Palani said, pursing her lips.

Ioane lowered the box of beads and bent down slightly. "Help me find a fertility bead, would you?"

"What are you trying to do to my daughter, Ioane? She is already with child."

"Who was the first to know she was with child?" Ioane asked defensively. "Her godmother is who. I still have my wits, even if everything else is failing. I am merely pairing the fertility bead with one of well-being to ensure a healthy birth," she explained.

Palani turned and picked through the contents of the box. "In that case, here's one." She took out a dark stone bead etched and painted with the silhouette of a pregnant woman in a thin white line. Ioane grabbed the bead between her finger and thumb.

"Bolin and Laksa are due soon," Ioane said. "That, along with Talia's, will make one-hundred and sixty-two. The most we have ever had."

"Pa'vil has been generous. The harvest was plentiful this year, and we will have more than enough food to feed all," Palani said.

"The Dai'akan is serving well."

"Yes, he is," Palani whispered. She watched a stream of children run past them, celebrating the return of the traders.

Ioane hummed softly and continued working on the bracelet.

～

A GUST of wind blew through the hut, and Masima shivered. His mind was calming but far from quiet. He had not heard anything from Pa'vil for several days, not unusual immediately following a feeding, but still disconcerting.

His thoughts floated towards Palani and Talia. He wondered what they were doing. *Talia is due soon.* His duty as the Dai'akan would keep him from knowing his grandchild, but he would observe from afar and celebrate in his way.

His thoughts drifted back to Pa'vil. Masima remembered his first time up on the mountain, scared but filled with awe at the prospect of serving his god. He had offered his blood after the oath, just as the Dai'akan's book had instructed. Pulling his arm from Pa'vil had felt like he was tearing his arm away from a shark's mouth. He had cried for a week in his hut afterward and dreaded Pa'vil's beckoning.

The Dai'akans' journals had outlined a series of meditations to help deal with the shock of the feedings. They centered on replaying the feedings of Pa'vil in his head, focusing on the experience. Some Dai'akans eschewed the meditations, their entries discussing the difficulty of concentrating and reliving such a horror. Others talked of reaching a place, an equilibrium, where the memories with Pa'vil were less troubling. One Dai'akan, Ruhi, had tallied up the years lived by all recorded Dai'akans from their journal entries and noted that those who practiced the meditations tended to write more and live longer.

The meditations that followed had been challenging. He struggled at first to control his breathing. Weeks into the practice, he had been on the verge of abandoning the meditations, but the experiences of previous Dai'akans strengthened his resolve, and he continued. Over several months, he noticed a gradual relaxing of his body and a clarity of the mind. The horrific memories had lessened their iron grip on his life, turning from ruminations to troubling thoughts. He still had occasional nightmares, waking drenched in sweat with his heart pounding through his chest and jaw aching, but he was better; he could enjoy food, take walks around the island, and, most importantly, write in his journal and engage with the Dai'akans yet to come, an army of descendants destined to maintain the wall between Arutua and the outside world.

The Elder's council knew enough to test for the Dai'akan, and they knew what he did, but the secrets of his job were just that—only the Dai'akan read the booklet and journals kept locked away. Only the Dai'akan knew Pa'vil's truth.

Masima exhaled slowly and went through visualizing feeding Pa'vil again. When his mind wandered, he went with it and gently brought the focus back to the feeding. Gentle winds pushed through his hut again and again. The bell rang in the distance. Masima barely noticed.

They come. My brothers come for me.

The thought hit Masima with such force that he opened his eyes and looked around his hut, searching for the speaker. Stark terror pushed through the link from Pa'vil. If Masima hadn't been meditating, he was sure he would be in a panic.

A series of images flashed before Masima. He ran in the dark, his breath ragged. *Pa'vil's memories.* He stopped at a cliff's edge, looking down at frothy waters lapping against the rock. The wind whipped up from below and almost blew him off his feet. He turned and saw an army of glowing eyes approaching. Something hot and bright shot past his cheek. He raised his hand to his face, then turned to the cliff and jumped. Cold water and darkness enveloped him.

He moved towards a light. His head burst out from the water's surface, and he gulped air, fighting against a raging current threatening to pull him down into a sleep he would not awaken from. His lungs burned. A rush of water slammed him against a rock. He latched on. The water receded, trying to tear him off, but he forced himself to climb. The frigid air assaulted him anew, a sweet and violent embrace. He retched sea water and then scanned his surroundings. He was perched on a tower of rock jutting out of the sea. His lips parted. He snarled and clutched the vial dangling from a chain around his neck. He yanked it off, bit into the glass, and leaned his head back. The taste of blood and fire filled his mouth. He swallowed. The fire moved through his body, into his muscles—pure otai.

The world went bright with rich colors raging around him. A moment of calmness caused him to look back toward the sea. A wall of water approached. *Death comes for me.* He laughed, then leaped with a surge of strength and rocketed into the sky. He looked down at the rock tower hit by a wall of seawater as he arced through the air with flailing arms and legs. He crashed into the cliff wall with a sickening crunch and collapsed onto a ledge. Suddenly, sharp pain coursed through his body as he felt bones snap back together and open wounds close. The bright colors of his vision blurred, then went black.

Masima opened his eyes. He was on the floor of his hut, drenched in sweat. He moved his hands. No pain. He coughed a couple of times, trying to force out the non-existent water from his lungs. The memory faded rapidly. Masima sat up. He never had visions that strong. Pa'vil had pulled him into one of his memories. Masima felt terror oozing through the link once more. A tingling traveled down his back.

They come.

The hunters with glowing eyes? How do I fight them? Masima stood, steadying himself against the wall, then grabbed his staff and dagger.

Bring me blood.

Masima thought of Palani, Talia, and his unborn grand-child and ran toward Arutua.

Talia could not suppress the smile as she approached Palani and Ioane. "They are arriving, Mother? Godmother?"

"Yes, there has been quite the commotion," Palani replied, gesturing to the beach where the villagers were gathered to watch the boats approach.

Talia walked as quickly as she could to the base of the stairs.

"I will help you down, godmother. Give me your other arm." She knew it was the wrong thing to say as soon as she glanced at her mom.

Ioane slapped Talia's arm away.

"Leave me be, child. Your mother's help is adequate for my purposes."

Talia hesitated and then took a step back.

"As you will, godmother."

When Palani and Ioane were off the steps, Ioane gestured for Talia's hand.

Talia offered her arm, and Ioane took a string of beads and slid it onto her wrist.

"This bracelet was made from beads dipped and etched in otai. The magic is strong and will help guide your child to a safe birth," Ioane said, patting Talia's hand.

"Thank you, godmother," she said.

Ioane fixed her with an intense stare. "The most dangerous action we take on this island is having a child, Talia. Take this bracelet off after your child is born."

Talia dipped her head. "I will do as you say."

Ioane patted Talia's hand. "Come, let us see the arrival of Kol'val. I am sure everyone on the island is eager."

IOANE KNEW something was wrong when the men on the boats did not return the customary shouts of greeting. The crowd parted for her. She went to the front and peered at the arriving canoes.

Talia and Palani stood back. "What is it, Mother? What does she see?" Talia whispered.

Palani shook her head. "I do not know. We will find out soon enough."

Ioane stood on the beach and spread her arms out wide. The waters surged up to her feet and then receded in the familiar rhythm of the tide. She turned around and spoke. Her voice carried through the silent crowd to Talia and Palani.

"There is a taint on the approaching boats. Pa'vil's commandments have been violated. They must be received as foreigners."

Kuresa, a stout young woman, stepped forward from the crowd.

"Elder Mother has spoken. Get back to defensive positions. Irutai, fetch the spears. Mura, ensure the children are gathered and safe in the Elder's hut."

Talia heard Ioane's words and went numb. *Tainted? Disobeyed Pa'vil's commandments? Who would do such a thing and jeopardize all they had built? Who would risk Pa'vil's wrath? Kol'val will make things right. Yes, he will bring the offender to justice.* Her mother led her away to the shade of the treeline, where others were gathering with weapons.

Masima arrived at the beach, running past Palani and Talia without breaking stride. He stopped at the water's edge, scrutinizing the approaching boats.

"I can feel it, Dai'akan, like oil on my skin," Ioane said. "Pa'vil is repulsed by the canoes." She stood next to him with her arms crossed and brow furrowed.

"I feel it too, but I do not see any foreigners on the boats.

They are our people to the last man. Perhaps it is something they carry?"

"Whoever broke our laws will answer for it," Ioane replied. The elder council will be strict."

Masima shook his head. "No, they will answer to Pa'vil directly. He has commanded it."

CHAPTER EIGHT

Zet awoke with a jolt on the cool stone floor and looked around in confusion. Another dungeon master had replaced Aatma. He remembered they'd been under attack, and he had spotted a group of intruders approaching the entrance, slaughtering his brothers and sisters. He'd felt a blinding rage building within and screamed at them from afar. Then he was lumbering forward, weaving between cacti, cursing at them. His tongue hadn't worked well, and he wasn't sure they under-stood his taunts because if they had, they would've faced him and died with honor so that he could feast on their brains.

He'd felt something slam into his back, and he crumpled to the ground. There was a sharp pain in his leg. Iseret had appeared at his side and placed a clawed hand on his shoulder as he struggled to rise.

"Wait, Zet," she'd said, "we will attack them when they are leaving and are weakest."

Zet had felt the warmth of her breath against his skin. *Iseret, so intelligent and good.* She'd taken one of his arms and put it around her shoulders. With her support, he'd returned to his feet and surveyed his surroundings. Zet could not say how much time had passed, but he'd felt an urgency to attack, such was the call from the dungeon. A tremendous explosion had sent him flying, and the link with Aatma was severed soon after. Zet had lain on the ground, staring into the dying light of Iseret's eyes, her scarred black lips twisted into a smile. "My Zet," she'd whispered, reaching out to him.

"Rise, my minions," said the voice of his new master. A familiar warmth infused Zet's body. He turned on his side and pushed himself up. His stomach lurched into his throat, and the room spun. A sharp pain, like a dagger twisting into his knee, caused his leg to buckle, and he collapsed onto the ground and moaned. Energy coursed through him from the core, and the pain abated. His vision focused, allowing him to study his surroundings. His leg was broken at the knee. To one side of him, a rat stood on its hind legs at attention, and on the other, a half-skeleton was propped up on its arms. Zet looked forward and saw the new master, a pale human with disheveled hair. Zet would not tolerate failure. He would stand with the others. With another moan, he pushed up from the ground once again.

The rat broke its gaze momentarily from Gabe and gave Zet a wary look, scooting away from him.

"Stop, Zap!" His master yelled, holding his hand out.

Zet got to a seated position and continued to struggle. He did not know who this Zap was, but if it didn't stop, it should be punished. *One must obey the master.*

Gabe pulled out a sheet of paper. "Zet, I mean. Stop, Zet."

Zet stopped. His new master had spoken his name. Aatma had never spoken his name. In truth, Zet's only interaction with Aatma was from a great distance when he was first summoned and linked with the horde. He was blessed to have this time with his new master.

"Really, it isn't necessary to stand. You can sit."

Zet did not move from his sitting position. He looked over at the rat and skeleton. They were all roughly at the same height. Equals. The master didn't want any of them to stand out. He was wise. Zet looked up at him in awe.

"You three," Gabe looked at each of them in turn, "have been tasked with protecting my dungeon from intruders. We will soon be powerful, but we are still building and vulnerable to attack. That is why it is of utmost importance that you do your job. Outside of this laboratory is a simple rectangle. You will each patrol that rectangle and attack anyone who tries to enter. Is that clear?"

Zet moaned, Moffet squeaked, and Clack clacked.

"I must go. Zet and Moffet, I will put some food and water out for you before I leave. If you need to relieve yourself, use the hole in the corner. Moffet and Clack, you will start your patrols. Zet, you..." Gabe trailed off as he looked at Zet, then around the laboratory. He noticed the broken glass on the floor underneath the table and remembered knocking something over after the joining. It must have been a large beaker. "You have a more important task," he continued. "You must pick up the broken glass on the floor and dump it in that hole over in the corner," he gestured.

Zet felt a surge of pride at being selected for the critical task. He moaned softly and began dragging himself across the floor to do as his master instructed.

Moffet zipped out the door and down the hallway without difficulty while Clack trailed, dragging its body. Gabe opened a bag of brain pellets, placed several handfuls on a metal saucer, and then put it on the floor next to Zet. He then emptied the bucket of water into the hole and refilled it, placing it next to the saucer.

"Good luck," his master said.

Zet nodded enthusiastically. He felt his master's gaze and a surge of pride. He would show his master how capable he was. Zet grabbed a shard of glass on the floor. Making his way towards the hole across the room, he tried to coordinate his elbow and knee while carrying the glass, but it became slick as he tightened his grip. There was a burning sensation in his hand. The image of Iseret came to his mind. She would tell him to focus on one movement at a time. The pain worsened, and Zet gritted his teeth. He paused his march. A viscous green liquid dripped down from the point of the glass shard, jutting out from the bottom of his hand. He was bleeding. *No matter what, I must show my master how strong I am.* He dropped the shard and picked it up with the other hand. The door to the laboratory closed with a loud thud. Zet looked back to find his master gone.

Zet felt a surge of energy. The bleeding from the deep gash in his hand slowed and stopped along with the pain. His strength returned, and he crossed the remainder of the laboratory, careful not to squeeze his hand too hard. He dropped the glass into the hole and moaned in approval at the sound of it clinking below. Zet lay next to the hole and rested. His hand itched fiercely, and he studied the gash as it closed. His knee had a similar itch.

A gurgling noise came from his stomach. Zet eyed the metal saucer on the other side of the transport circle and crawled back over. He ate a mouthful of brain pellets. They were dry and dusty. He plunged his head into the bucket beside the saucer and drank water. When he had finished eating all the pellets, he looked at the bits of glass, most no more significant than a pebble, spread out beneath the tables. *There is a better way.* A strange calm came over Zet. His mouth hung open, and he felt an unfamiliar and pleasant sensation like a flower opening up to the sun. He closed his eyes and dreamed of cleaning Aatma's dungeon. When he awoke, he grabbed the empty metal saucer and went to the glass, a dim light glowing in his eyes.

~

"Maybe I can get my money back?" Gabe paced back and forth while Miranda sat watching him from her desk. "What was I thinking?" He stopped and turned to face her, wringing his hands. "It was pathetic, Miranda, watching it crawl and bleed across the floor. There's no way it can defend the dungeon. No way."

"Gabe, try to relax. Drink some of your tea. It has the dark, Lassian honey you like."

He walked over to the table and picked up the saucer and cup. They trembled in his hand. "That banshee and ball of light at the consignment shop swindled me. I'm sure of it."

"Yesterday, you praised them, and now you think you were tricked?"

"I don't know. I frequent other shops. Maybe word got out that I was looking for minions and desperate?" He took a sip of his tea.

"Look at where you are, brother. You've joined with your dungeon and have minions patrolling as we speak. Actual minions. Think about how many have failed before getting to where you are today. You have to focus on making and selling potions. Then you can buy new minions from a reputable summoner and get your ring back. It's what you've been saying. This doesn't change anything."

"But if I'm attacked, Miranda. Master Ezil even said, with the Empress sponsoring a new generation of dungeon masters, there's going to be a surge of adventurers. With a few swipes of a sword, my minions would be dispatched, and then they'd come for me...." He put his hand over his heart, "I would be ripped from the energy core and wish I had died in the outlands fighting for the Empress. The light illuminate her," he mumbled. "Where's Colin when you need him? He'd get a good laugh out of this." Gabe swallowed the last of the tea and faced his sister.

"Forget Colin. What are their names?" Miranda asked.

"Who?"

"The minions. What are their names?

"Minions?" Gabe shook his head in confusion. "Minions? Miranda, what does it matter?"

She rolled her eyes and sighed. "Just tell me their names."

Gabe fumbled for the sheet in his pocket. "The rat's name is Moffet; the skeleton is Clack, and the zombie is Zet. So?"

"You're already in better shape than most when they start. Remember your training and think strategically. Use what you have. Moffet can move quickly and bite. Clack can grab and be helpful in the laboratory. Zet can grab and tear." Miranda paused to cough into her handkerchief. "This worry is just noise. And I believe," she said with a raised finger between coughs, "those shop minions told you the truth."

Gabe had been so caught up in the weaknesses of his minions that he had never bothered to think about their strengths. He reached out to his dungeon and felt his minions moving about. He felt one running down the corridor, the light pitter-patter of its feet against the dungeon skin on the floor. *There's Moffet.* A much slower presence was near the entrance dragging itself across the bottom of the stairs. *That would be Clack. And Zet? Why isn't he moving to clean up the glass? Maybe he's eating.* Gabe dismissed them from his mind.

"Do you ever get tired of being right all the time?"

"Not really."

"You should be here in my place. Not me."

"Find that cure, Gabe, and I will come work with you." Miranda coughed again.

"I will do my best. Thank you for feeding me," he said, kissing her forehead.

"Back to your dungeon so soon?"

"I'm headed off to check the available contracts to see if there is any low-hanging fruit. I need to make money."

"You know what you might be able to do?"

Gabe saw the twinkle in his sister's eye. "What? What is it?"

"You should stop by the University and see if Professor Galdon has a contract that needs filling. You might get something more lucrative."

"Oh, that's a great idea. I avoid guild competition by contracting directly with a university. Brilliant!" There were few exceptions to seeking contracts outside of guild purview, but education was one of them.

Miranda beamed theatrically at her brother's praise, then doubled over in a coughing fit.

"I'm going to stop talking to you before you turn inside out," Gabe said, frowning.

Miranda had been right, of course. Professor Galdon had been eager to help, stating that her seniors had practicums in just under a fortnight and that she would gladly pay a silver mark for each resin. Gabe left the Professor with a contract for two dozen firelime resins.

While walking back to his dungeon, Gabe recalled his practicums. Time slowed when you sat in lectures, toiled away in labs, and took tests. He'd been out of school for over a year, but it felt like a lifetime. His closest friends had decided against entering the Great Game. Instead, they pursued other jobs, joined their family business, or decided to further their studies. Only Gabe had remained, and he had just scored his first contract.

CHAPTER NINE

Kol'val and Tamar left the traders at the canoes and marched up the beach with slow purpose. Returning to Arutua had always been a festive affair, filled with ceremony and jubilation as the elder council accepted them once more into Pa'vil's arms, but this reception was different. Family and friends stood in shadows with grim faces, bows in hand, and spears strapped across their backs. The villagers had somehow known that Pa'vil's laws were broken and had met them as potential enemies. They stopped well short of the trees. Kol'val did not doubt that if he made a wrong step, he would be met with an arrow through the chest.

"State the betrayal," Ioane commanded.

Tamar took a step forward. "Kol'val entered the city," he said.

Ioane and the Dai'akan advanced to meet them. Ioane held Masima's arm to stabilize her footing on the uneven yellow sand. They were an odd pair; the Dai'akan with his lean, muscular build, peppered gray hair down to his shoulders, and a face unyielding as marble, while Ioane barely reached his waist, bent over with a dozen necklaces swinging and jangling as she walked. Her long, white hair was braided and barely swung with her small steps. She peered up at Kol'val and Tamar and back at Masima after Tamar spoke, shaking her head in sadness. They stopped well short of the traders.

"Tamar and Kol'val advance to us," Ioane said.

When they complied, Ioane turned to Kol'val, disappointment tinging her voice, "I did not expect this from you."

The Dai'akan stood like a statue studying Kol'val, then spoke, "What have you brought, Kol'val? What disease have you...."

Ioane held up her hand.

"We are not there yet, Dai'akan. Formalities must be adhered to," Ioane said. She turned towards Tamar. "Has Kol'val done or said anything that would taint others?"

"No, island mother, he has not. When he returned, he was stripped of his command and has not spoken of what he has seen."

"What does Kol'val bring with him that does not belong?" Ioane asked.

"He brought a dagger, island mother," Tamar replied.

A hiss escaped the Dai'akan's lips.

"Why was it permitted?" Ioane asked.

Kol'val pulled an object wrapped in cloth from his belt and held it out. The Dai'akan took the package in his hand and unwrapped it. He and Ioane gasped simultaneously, and the Dai'akan nearly dropped the weapon, such was his shock.

"Now you see. I could not refuse the return of a holy relic," Kol'val said.

Ioane closed her eyes with a soft prayer to Pa'vil emanating from her lips. Kol'val was pleased by their surprise. He wanted to point at the dagger and tell them that he had acted to protect the island and his people, but he did not have permission to speak freely and knew that if he did, it would only weaken his case.

Kol'val looked to the Dai'akan and flinched at the intensity of his stare.

"Is there anything else you would like to add, Tamar?" Ioane asked.

"I know nothing more," Tamar replied.

"Go," Ioane said. "Wait with your men. They are forbidden from entering the village until the Elders meet. Is that clear?"

"Yes, island mother," Tamar said. He left Kol'val alone with Ioane and the Dai'akan.

Ioane waited until he was out of earshot before speaking. "There is but the Dai'akan and I to listen to your words and judge what you have done, Kol'val. Speak the truth."

Kol'val didn't hold anything back. He told them of the ultimatum at the docks, the Mahajeen's sickness, the Empress, and her war of expansion. Finally, he spoke of the soul dagger, a weapon from Pa'vil that could protect the island.

Ioane listened with curiosity while the Dai'akan folded his arms with a scowl that seemed to darken with the telling.

When Kol'val finished, Ioane turned to the Dai'akan. "What of the dagger?" she said.

"The dagger appears identical to mine, but the weight and glow are off. This dagger has been defiled and does not belong."

Kol'val felt as if his insides had been sucked out of his body. There was only despair.

"Yes," Ioane said, pointing at the dagger, "a fine trap, this... thing. Your pride has obscured your judgment, Kol'val. You have decided our fate as if you were the Dai'akan. If the Mahajeen had rejected us as trading partners, we would have survived returning to the old ways. You have taken that choice from us."

"We are being hunted," the Dai'akan said, placing the dagger back in its cloth. "You have marked us and disgraced yourself by bringing this abomination here. Ioane is right. You were blinded by honor. What of your family? Of Talia and your unborn child? Did you not think of them."

"I did it *for them*," Kol'val said. "To protect Talia and your grandchild."

The Dai'akan's face twisted in rage.

Ioane placed a hand on the Dai'akan's forearm. "I do not doubt that it started that way, Kol'val," she said, "but you saw glory in taking up that dagger, and now you must seek penance in its destruction."

"Give me a boat," Kol'val said. "I will take it far from here and lure them away. Let my death have meaning."

The Dai'akan mumbled and looked back at the mountain, shaking his head. "There is no time. What I do Pa'vil has decreed. Your fate is decided." He rewrapped the blade and handed it to Kol'val. "It is your burden to carry."

After experiencing Pa'vil's memory in the hut, Masima was hesitant to communicate any thought that didn't appease Pa'vil, fearing it would trigger another intense flashback, leaving him incapacitated. He wondered how many Dai'akans had fallen victim to a sudden thought or desire from Pa'vil while climbing or swimming. How many deaths or injuries resulted from Pa'vil's intrusive whims? Masima focused on his breathing, trying to calm himself.

They left Kol'val alone on the beach between the traders and the villagers. He no longer belonged to either group. Standing with Ioane in the shade of the trees while she talked with some of the elders, Masima studied Kol'val, whose face was buried in his hands. *You will know of Pa'vil's appetite soon enough.* His mind drifted to Mahajeen. *How had he encountered such a dagger and known it would tempt Kol'val?* He needed time to think.

"Dai'akan!" Ioane's voice broke his concentration. She crossed the gap between them and peered up at him with concern. "Your advice on a potential evacuation would be appreciated. Can you stay to meet with the elders?"

Masima shook his head. "I must go right away," he replied. "Pa'vil may still protect us if he is appeased."

She nodded and looked at the lone figure standing on the beach. "What of him?"

Masima hesitated. To know Pa'vil's desire for blood was forbidden to all save the Dai'akan.

"Kol'val has sealed his fate and mine. Pa'vil may decide to come down from the mountain. Prepare for the Swell."

Ioane spoke in a forced whisper, "You are sure, Dai'akan? The intruders have not yet arrived. Perhaps they will not."

"Pa'vil will answer soon enough. Know that when the Swell begins, there will be no mercy."

Ioane's head sank, and Masima noticed the tears staining the sand beneath her.

"We will do as Pa'vil commands," Ioane said. She turned and walked back to the gathering of elders.

They come. Without my strength, this island will die—hack at the roots, and the tree rots. Bring me the blood of three so that I may rise.

Masima leaned against the nearest tree, breathing raggedly. In the journals, when Pa'vil was not fed, the vegetation browned, and people got sick. Pa'vil spoke the truth. He was the heart of the island. Without him, the island would die. But the memory Masima had borne witness to had shown Pa'vil fleeing the hunters. Could he withstand their power?

They are many. You are but one. Will it be enough? Masima pushed the thought across that barrier on the edge of its consciousness, knowing that what he asked was near blasphemy.

YOU QUESTION ME? You will die, bag of blood. You and everything you know.

If Masima had not been leaning on the tree, his knees would have buckled at the torrent of anger from Pa'vil. When his god had finished his rant, Masima stepped away from the tree, standing tall. He looked around, and his eyes fell on Talia and Palani standing far off in the trees near the village. Palani, his kind and loving wife, was leaning close and comforting Talia while rubbing her back. Talia would pay the highest price of them all. She would lose her husband and unborn child.

Pa'vil's anger came again, but Masima withstood the wave of emotion. He glanced up Mount Laiya, then to his daughter. Talia's body shook while she sobbed, her hands cupping her chin in despair. Masima saw his future in her, and with it, a plan formed. *I will come, and I will bring Kol'val and Talia with me.*

CHAPTER TEN

Zet sat in the transport circle, tracing the symbols with a finger. He had always been drawn to the odd little symbols. In Aatma's dungeon, he remembered moving heavy boxes into circles like this one with Ivan the shambler. Whenever they finished early, Zet would walk the periphery of the circle and study the shapes while Ivan paced the room, heavy cords of muscle twitching over his immense body. Inevitably, Zet would be ordered back outside to patrol. He would tell Iseret about his work in the pyramid with hand gestures and grunts.

A creaking sound came from the entrance. His master walked in and heaved a basket onto the table with a grunt. The basket was tan and made of wide, interwoven pieces of wicker. The light of the dungeon wall hit a part of the basket just right, and it shone like gold. Zet followed that piece of wicker as it passed above and below other pieces, mesmerized by its complexity.

Gabe looked over at Zet in the transport circle and

frowned. "I felt your injury drawing on the energy core. Your leg looks better."

Zet moaned.

Gabe rolled his eyes. "Do try and stand," he said.

Zet stood with difficulty, his knee holding some weight.

"Come away from the transport circle," he said. "They can be dangerous."

Zet was puzzled by his master's words. *How could transport circles be dangerous?* He had spent much time in one without any problems.

"You may have a permanent limp." Gabe opened his mouth as if to say something, then closed it and sighed. "I've invested in you, Zep. I hope you're worthy."

Zet searched the room for another creature named Zep.

"I see you cleaned up all of the glass. How did you do it?"

Zet picked up the metal saucer and made a scooping motion.

"Smart," Gabe said as he bit into a sandwich.

Zet breathed deeply, feeling his chest expand, and groaned at his master's compliment.

"Go out and patrol with the others. Shut the door behind you, and don't disturb me."

Zet did as he was asked while Gabe set about preparing his laboratory. He took down "The Principles of Potion-Making: Volume II" from the long shelf behind him and flipped through the pages while eating, familiarizing himself with the firelime resin Professor Galdon had ordered. No food was allowed in the University laboratories, and Gabe felt a certain freedom in seeing crumbs fall onto the table. From the top shelf, he grabbed a jar of calcium carbonate, ignis regia, Labularia Majus paste, and a tincture of lime before arranging them on the table in the order in which he would need them. He removed the stopper on the tincture of lime and sniffed its contents and coughed. It had lost none of its potency since he had bought it a year earlier.

He felt the veins of energy flowing along the dungeon's walls, following them down into the waste incinerator and then up to the scrubbers and burners in the hoods venting into the field above. The scrubbers wouldn't eradicate the cooking smell completely, but they made it less likely that a band of roving adventurers would pick up the scent.

Time melted away as he worked. The difficulty wasn't in making the resin itself. Sure, one could boil off too much alcohol and decrease the flammability of the compound or fail to add enough of the flower Labularia Majus at the right moment, rendering the resin useless as it sloughed off its intended target. Those were mistakes Gabe was trained to avoid.

What worried him were minor changes in his new laboratory; the ambient energy and temperature, the quality of his ingredients, and the accuracy of his measuring devices. Any one error would likely have a minimal impact, but when stacked together, they could cripple his ability to cook for days, if not weeks, as he tracked down each culprit. And it wasn't like these errors went away. As the potions grew in complexity, so did his need for precision and accuracy.

When he filled a glass flask and ventured outside to test the resin, he wasn't surprised to find that the resin barely stuck to the base of a tree and took a full three seconds to light with a torch. Standing in the darkness with his arms folded and head shaking, Gabe kicked some earth over the anemic fire and returned to his laboratory. He had work to do.

The attack came at twilight, with the sun's last glow turning the scattered clouds on the horizon into fiery cotton balls. Gabe had been so busy testing his resin that he failed to pull the strings on the dungeon door cover when returning. As he hunched over his table working, he heard a muffled shout from the field above. His worst fears were confirmed when Moffet ran through the slightly open door, sat on its haunches, and squeaked furiously at him. The dungeon had been spotted. Gabe realized his mistake. He had left the door uncovered. He wanted to run to the entrance, pull the strings, and cover the door, but it was too late. He stared through the rat and saw the destruction of everything he had built play out before him. His face paled, and the dungeon dimmed around him. Tears filled his eyes. "I'm going to die. Don't leave me," he said, looking at the rat.

Moffet squeaked.

THE MASTER HAD DROPPED the light level of the dungeon. *A wise decision.* He stood with Clack at the bottom of the stairs and wondered when the master would give commands. He heard the slamming of the laboratory door and a loud click. The master did not want to be bothered.

Two days of Zet walking in circles around the dungeon with Clack and Moffet had brought progress. For one, Clack had taught Zet to count up to ten using his fingers. For two, they had worked on simple directional commands with each other so they could coordinate during an attack. Zet made three soft clicks with his teeth as he counted the different voices. He looked down at Clack, whose two red eyes bobbed up and down while it dragged itself across the dungeon skin. *Where was Moffet?* Three intruders against one and a half defenders. That fight did not seem fair.

He thought back to the battles of his previous dungeon, of the shambler's mighty roar signaling that intruders had made it to the pyramid. Iseret used to say, "These adventurers all have a plan until they hear a shambler roar," and she was right. On several occasions, moments after hearing the shambler, the adventurers would come running out of the pyramid, dodging past Zet and Iseret, and retreating to the forest.

He looked over at Clack. The skeleton sat up against the stone wall at an oblique angle, struggling to stay upright. He wondered how they would fight. They did not have a shambler to protect them. Zet moaned loudly, louder than he had meant to. His voice echoed down the halls. He moaned again and listened to his echo. He gestured to Clack, and they moved down the hallway, deeper into the dungeon.

~

"WE'RE NOT DOING THIS," Riz said. "My energy stone is 10%, and Simon is drunk."

Simon scoffed. "I might be a wee bit buzzed, but djunk?" He leaned forward to challenge any objection before stumbling to catch himself.

Maye rolled her eyes. Her short, red hair bounced with her quick head movements. "Our map was just updated. There's no mention of this dungeon. The field is clean, a couple of light tracks is all. We are dealing with fresh meat, Riz, ripe for the picking. We could get enough money to charge your stone fully. Wouldn't it be nice not to worry about your magic source for a while?"

Simon pointed at Maye. "What she said. Plus, we get to kill minions and a halfwit." He made a stabbing motion with his swordless hand. "Would be nice to see some blood."

"Good points, Maye," Riz said, ignoring the frown on Simon's face. She was tired of just getting by, of scrounging just enough money to put a trickle of energy into her stone. The prospect of having a full charge was almost enough to make her giddy, but greed made people reckless and got them killed. "What if it's a trap?" She asked. "What if other adventurers saw this opportunity and thought the same? It isn't on any map, and we are close to a major city? Isn't that strange? What if we walk in and are attacked on all sides by a horde of zombies or a nest of arachnoids?"

Simon waved off Riz's protestations. "What if this, what if that? Nonsense. All of it. I can smell a trap a mile off, and this ain't it. Maye and I say 'yes,' and you say 'nay.' That's two to one. TWO to ONE. I will take a piss, and when I get back, we attack." He marched off into the trees.

Maye took a step closer and put her hand on Riz's shoulder. "At least he didn't try to pull rank based on age this time and go off about hemorrhoids and back pain." Simon was a good twenty years older than Maye and Riz and had often lorded that over them. "The Empress is funding all of these new dungeon masters, remember? I hate to say it, but Simon is right. Look, if we detect any funny business, we are out. If the monsters are above our level, we are out. Caution will be our guide." Maye brushed Riz's cheek. "We need this."

"What about Simon?" Riz said. "Caution has never been his guide."

Maye could tell she had won over Riz. "He'll take point," she said with a smirk.

Simon came back from the horses with a hammer in his hand. "There's too much excitement for me to pee. That's all right. I don't plan on this battle taking too long. We ready?"

Maye looked over at Riz. They nodded in unison.

"That's more like it," Simon said, walking to the entrance. He began pounding away at the dungeon door when Maye called on him to stop.

"I was just getting started," he said between breaths.

"Those are quality doors, Simon. We could get good money

for them. If the cover is off, it stands to reason that the doors could be open."

Simon shrugged. "You can try, but no one...."

His voice trailed off, and the hammer dropped from his grasp as Maye bent down and pulled back one of the doors, revealing the steps leading down into the dungeon.

"Dragon's spit," Simon said.

"What did I say, Riz? That's new dungeon skin. After you, Simon," Maye gestured towards the opening.

"I think we bloody well know what we're dealing with here," Simon replied.

"Riz, you take up the rear. Defensive spell, please."

"Air shield activated," Riz said with a wave of her arms. The core hanging from her necklace glowed a soft blue. "Should I activate the memory crystal?"

"The guild may frown on us if we don't. How many do you have?" Maye asked.

"Just the one."

Simon felt a gust and reached out to touch the thickened air hovering before he pulled out his sword and descended the stairs with a loud belch.

Maye shook her head. "Save it for another time. We could be a laughing stock depending on how this goes." She followed behind and quietly cursed Simon, her hand flapping back and forth as the stench of digested boiled chicken and mead accosted her.

They were halfway down the hall on the right side when they heard a series of deep guttural sounds, like a demon-hound hacking up a human femur. Simon paused mid-walk and looked behind him at Maye and then Riz. "What the hell was that?" Riz asked. She looked behind her, ready to cast another air shield in case a minion tried a surprise attack from behind.

"Not sure," Simon said, frowning. He looked back to Maye. "Any idea?"

"Not to worry, probably just a dungeon wolf," Maye replied, nudging Simon. "You've killed a dozen of them. This is no different." Simon began moving forward again but at a decidedly slower pace.

The noise grew louder as they advanced. A shadow flickered against the wall before them, and they froze. There was a loud crunching sound, and then a skeleton, or half of one, crashed against the wall in front of them. It looked up at them, its red eyes dimming, and stretched out a hand as if asking for help before slumping onto the ground, motionless. "Ogre piss," Simon muttered. Maye looked back at Riz inching backward, her energy stone gleaming bright blue around her neck as she drew in more energy to prepare for another spell.

That's when they heard the roar, a bellow from down the hallway that seemed to grate against the very skin of the dungeon, reverberating through the hallway. Simon screamed, and the smell of piss hung thick in the air.

It's coming for us. Riz struggled to fight against the panic bubbling up. She pulled more energy from her stone and began moving her arms. Water condensed in front of Simon, and thin needles of ice shot down the hallway, passing over the skeleton's still body and sticking into the dungeon skin on the other side. *Oh, Empress Inalda, help us.*

Another roar came. The shadows on the wall danced before them as something colossal moved. "Shambler," Simon muttered under his breath. He looked back at Maye and Riz. "That be a shambler."

With the echo of the roar dying, a distinctive crack sounded. Riz's eyes rolled back into her head. She slumped against the dungeon wall and slid down. Her stone had shattered and hung dark and ruined around her neck. She had drawn too much energy. The dungeon hallway glowed bright around them as the energy she had been holding seeped from her grasp and was absorbed into the walls.

Maye yelled for help. Simon grabbed the back of Riz's coat while Maye took her legs. They retreated up the stairs, stumbling as they went. Maye and Simon threw Riz over her horse, scrambled up on their own, and galloped into the night.

CHAPTER ELEVEN

Just below the deck of the Stork lay the ship's main sleeping quarters, an ample space made visible by the light of lanterns lining its periphery. Hammocks were arranged in rows across the main cabin. Beetle lay in his hammock, listening to several men talk while he watched the diffuse shadows dance across the ceiling. He was worried about the ship's crew. Tensions were running high with the impending invasion, and what had once been whispers of concern or conjecture; now skirted rebellion.

"Think of it, five bloody mages with enough power I'd wager to blow this ship to bits," Herald said. "Makes the skin crawl. What're we doing here?" He propped himself up on his elbow and gave the men around him a challenging eye. "I heard them chanting the other night before lights out. Right below us. I don't know how much more we can take?"

A few nods and grunts said others had heard the chanting and agreed.

Beetle had always disliked Herald. He'd smile to your face and talk behind your back. A fellow like that could spoil an entire crew, given a few months. It'd be best to drop him off at the nearest island with a sword and a prayer or slit his throat and be done with it.

"We've got a right to know what's going on," Herald added, hitting his fist on the wood floor. "The Captain's a good man. But who knows what the mages are doing to him?"

A louder series of nods and grunts followed.

"You don't know what we're doing, eh?" Beetle said with his hands tucked behind his head. Silence. They had thought him asleep. "Sounds to me like you're saying Captain Ryall doesn't know what he's doing, that he's a puppet for them mages? Is that the face of it, Herald?"

"I ain't saying that," Herald replied. "There seems to be a bit of confusion. It feels like we're in the dark on this one. When we gonna know what's going on?"

"When the Captain tells us," Beetle replied. "What he's doing is putting gold in our pockets. That's why you're here, Herald."

"What good is gold if I'm dead, Beetle? Or worse, mad, like that loon in the crow's nest? It's the mages who did that to him. I'm sure of it."

More nods and grunts followed Herald's challenge.

Beetle sat up and swung his legs over the side. He looked out at the men; Herald, with his crooked mouth and a puffy scar running down the right cheek, looked away from Beetle's probing gaze; Horsel and Orvin, Finn and Crow, wouldn't meet his eye. They were scared. Beetle felt that same fear in the pit of his stomach, but he had learned to push it down long ago. Fear like that only gums you up and kills you when you're in a pinch.

"I get it," Beetle said. "I don't like mages on the ship any more than you do, but a contract was signed in good faith. Put aside the fairytales of your youth and put your trust in the

Captain. He's earned it. Besides, what are you going to do, Herald? March down there and tell the mages no deal? That we are returning, and they should leave us be? You say you might not live to spend the gold. I say you're in the wrong line of work if that's your worry."

There was a long pause before Herald responded. "I don't like it, Beetle. A man has the right not to like something and speak up. It's a right."

"Yes, Herald. You can say you don't like something, but if I see any action against the Captain, it ain't going to be the mages you need to worry about. Now, go to sleep."

Herald retreated into his hammock in silence. The others followed his lead.

Beetle drifted to sleep after some time, but his dreams troubled him.

When Beetle walked out on deck the following morning for shift change, the madman's cackles drifted down, pelting him like hail.

"I wish he'd shut up," Beetle whispered to himself. He looked around to see if anyone had heard him and saw Leonid approaching.

"The man up in the crow's nest just started pointing west," Leonid said.

"Does the Captain know?"

"Not yet. I didn't want to wake him."

"Get some rest, kid. I'll notify him when the new shift is in a rhythm."

Other men stumbled up behind Beetle from below deck, bleary-eyed and ready for the morning.

"Oye!" Beetle yelled, "let's get a move on!" As if time had suddenly started again, the men coming off shift broke away from their duties and rushed down behind Beetle while the fresh crew went to work.

Beetle was about to visit the Captain when he heard gasps from a few crew members. The mages emerged from below deck cloaked in heavy wool. He did not dare look long; it was said that a mage could boil your blood with a stare, and he liked his blood just the way it was. The crew focused on their work, trying hard to ignore the mages in their midst, but Beetle felt it; the crew's sanity was slipping.

"We've got a busy day ahead of us," he yelled. "Let's keep our wits about us." He gave Herald a hard stare before marching to the Captain's quarters and rapping on the door.

Talia had started arguing with Kol'val at the base of Mount Laiya as Masima led with his staff. It had been a long while since Masima had been around people for any length of time, and he quickly grew exasperated by Talia's invectives and Kol'val's pleas. He ordered them to keep quiet and concentrate on the path, reminding them they would need energy for the challenging climb ahead.

At first, Talia had asked for Masima's help, eschewing Kol'val's offers. Still, when the thick surrounding vegetation gave way to patches of grass and lichen-covered boulder fields, she acquiesced and let both Masima and Kol'val assist her in scrambling over the black rock. At some point, the energy between Talia and Kol'val shifted. Kol'val began whispering words of encouragement to her, and his hands lingered on Talia. She would thank him with a smile or touch him in return. Masima had found it all annoying and could have stopped it with a command, but he owed Talia a respite from the tribulations she would soon face.

They hiked through the night, using the light of Masima's staff to light the way when needed. "He awaits us," Masima said, pointing to the stone building on the island when they reached the top and entered the caldera. The cool air of morning was calm. Masima shivered. It had nothing to do with the cold.

Kol'val turned to Talia, who had collapsed against the rock, sweaty and pale, with a blank stare that said she had been pushed too far. Kol'val caressed her face and leaned in to whisper in her ear.

They had made it, despite the glacial pace. He pulled a water skin from his bag and handed it to Kol'val, who urged Talia to drink. The day was clear, and the yellow circle sat in a band of red that gave way to a band of white before yielding to the crisp blue of the clear sky. *My last sunrise.* He wondered if he had ever truly appreciated its beauty before.

He called Kol'val over. "Your vision is keener than mine," he said. "Do you see any boats from the direction of the city?"

They stood still for a long moment, scanning the horizon for some trace of the enemy.

"I do not," Kol'val finally said.

Masima did not see anything either. "We may have arrived in time," he said.

It must be destroyed.

Masima wasn't sure if it was his thought or Pa'vil's. He took the water skin from Kol'val's hands, walked over to Talia, and dumped what remained over her. Talia shook her head and looked up at him.

"I'm sorry, Father," she muttered.

Talia would run up to him as a little girl and wrap her arms around his leg, yelling, "I've got you, father. I won't let go." He did not bury the memory. Instead, he embraced it, studying how he was content with a family. She was almost a stranger to him now.

"It is time for you to say your goodbyes. Kol'val, I will come and get you when I am ready."

Masima went to the pool's edge and peered at his reflection in the sparkling otai. A slight gust blew, turning his reflection fuzzy. He stepped away and left Talia and Kol'val alone as he walked across the bridge and into the mausoleum. His staff and dagger flared to life in the darkness. Pa'vil lay on the stone slab, as he always did, emaciated, unmoving.

We are here. What would you have me do?

Bring me the villagers.

I will bring you one. The other will wait.

Bring me blood, Dai'akan. Do your job.

Masima left his staff against the wall and walked back out to find Kol'val embracing Talia as she sat on the ground.

"Do not be afraid. Pa'vil calls for you, Kol'val." Masima said.

Kol'val kissed Talia, then whispered again in her ear and stood. He let go of her hand and walked to Masima.

"Follow me. Do what I say and do not speak."

Kol'val's eyes were wide, and his head trembled in the soft light. Masima remembered when he first saw Pa'vil and tried to think of some encouraging words. "Your redemption is at hand," was all he could muster.

"Go to the other side of Pa'vil. Kneel as I kneel. Do as I do."

Masima worked quickly. He cut Pa'vil's hand, then bade Kol'val put his hand out and did the same. Kol'val, to his credit, did not flinch as the sharp blade sliced into his flesh. He put their hands together, and they joined. Kol'val screamed and writhed in pain while Pa'vil's eyes glowed as he fed. Masima studied Kol'val with a morbid fascination. *This is what I must look like.* Kol'val's writhing turned into convulsions. He tried to pull away at some point but was too weak to separate. Finally, his eyes rolled into the back of his head, and he slumped over on the stone, dead.

Pa'vil's mouth parted, and his tongue darted out, licking at his lips. "More," he said weakly. Masima had never heard Pa'vil speak. He stood and backed away. Pa'vil's eyes shone bright, and he turned his head, watching Masima.

Bring me more.

The thought thundered in Masima's head. Pa'vil was stronger than Masima had ever seen him. He went around to Kol'val's body and picked up the dagger wrapped in cloth. "You must destroy the object first," he said.

Bring me another. I am still too weak. We die if I cannot fight.

Destroy the object now, or I will leave, and they will come for you.

Pa'vil's upper lip lifted in a snarl as he followed Masima's movements.

He opened the cloth, placed the hilt in Pa'vil's hands, and moved away. Pa'vil's snarl turned into a grimace. He began chanting through clenched teeth. The muscles of his hands grew taut, squeezing the grip of the dagger. The chant grew louder, and his voice reverberated as if coming from every direction, filling the small space. Masima covered his ears. With the rising volume of Pa'vil's voice, the light from the dagger's pommel clutched in his hands intensified, escaping through the cracks of his tightly wrapped fingers. He heard a scream from Pa'vil and then a sound like the squashing of a plump fruit. The bright light of the dagger blinked out of existence, and copious amounts of blood and tissue spilled from Pa'vil's hands as if the dagger's hilt had held the innards of an entire person. Pa'vil's fingers parted, and the remains of the dagger clattered to the floor, its hilt in ruins. A fetid smell like rotting flesh hung in the air. Masima stepped outside into the fresh air to avoid retching, leaving Pa'vil on the cold slab.

~

BEETLE PRACTICALLY BARGED into the Captain's quarters, telling him about the madman cackling from above and Elendr and the mages strutting around the deck as if they owned the ship. "You need to be out there," Beetle said. The appearance of being in command was necessary, even if it wasn't entirely true. Captain Ryall agreed and paused his morning writing routine to follow Beetle onto the deck.

"The mages tell me that we are getting close. We will likely be at our destination today," Elendr said, greeting the Captain. The mages were thin figures clothed in cowls, like emaciated monks, and stood back from Elendr, huddled together.

"My men and I are ready, Elendr." The Captain's eyes lingered on the mages. "We don't want any surprises," he said.

"Nor do we. I have complete confidence in your abilities, Captain. I hope the feeling is reciprocated."

Without warning, a screech came from above, followed by a loud pop. The Captain felt a warm spray on his face and wondered how it could rain with a clear sky. He turned to ask what had happened and found Beetle's face covered in blood, staring back at him. They both looked up and saw bits of flesh dripping from the crow's nest. A large piece splatted next to where Beetle stood.

"Well," Beetle said, wiping blood from his face, "at least he shut up."

CHAPTER TWELVE

Sitting beside the locked door with his knees folded, Gabe clutched a book on fungi and their uses in the laboratory. How a book was to stop a sword, Gabe did not know. Moffet stood in front of the door and hissed. Gabe had given the rat the command to defend him with its life. He heard a crash and a deep rumble. What felt like a giant's hand wrapped around his heart and squeezed. His hands went numb, and inky blotches danced across his vision. Covered in sweat, he tried to breathe and think, but his only company was the rhythmic pounding of his heartbeat raging in his ears and the numerous permutations of his imminent death playing in his thoughts. The screams of terror in the distance confirmed his fears. He went still. Death would not be long, he thought.

But death did not come. After what seemed an eternity, his senses began to return. At first, the tingling of the skin on his forearms and the color in his vision, then, a torrent; the smell of resin, sour and pungent, filling his nostrils, the aching of muscles long congealed demanding movement, and the awareness of the dungeon, always there in the back of his mind. Gabe sensed the varying pressures on the dungeon skin, his skin. There were no heavy footsteps or motionless bodies. Clack and Zet patrolled the halls as if nothing were amiss. He turned his attention to the energy core, thinking the power source had faltered, but it pulsed at full power, the drain of the past few days all but erased.

He had felt the intruders entering the dungeon and had heard their shouts and screams. *Where were they?* He inched up the wall to a standing position and opened his hands. They ached with the effort. He released a series of breaths and placed the book on the table before him. Gabe turned and pulled the key from his pocket. He fumbled with the lock in his trembling, clammy hands until the key turned. He heard a soft click. Peering out into the darkness, Gabe squinted. He could barely make out a form turning the corner. He knew it to be Zet. He could feel the zombie's plodding footsteps on the floor. Still, his imagination replaced his minion with an intruder trying to lure him out of the laboratory with a concealing spell. Gabe pulled energy from the core and out into the pulsing veins traveling beneath the dungeon's skin. The light flared. He could distinguish the back of Zet's patchy head and the tattered clothes hanging limply from his form.

"Zet," he managed in a whisper. The minion turned and looked at his master beckoning to him. Zet approached, his yellow complexion springing to life in the light. "Where are the intruders?" Gabe asked.

Zet moaned and made several hand motions, then stood still. Gabe tried to make sense of the zombie's gesticulations. He opened the door fully and looked around, daring some adventurer with a longsword to rush at him from the shadows.

He turned his attention back to Zet. "I don't understand."

He searched Zet's face as if he could divine the answer from the zombie's sallow cheeks and jaundiced eyes.

Zet put his hands to his mouth and made a sound. Gabe's eyes went wide. It was the deep rumble he had heard through the door. A pressure rose in his chest, threatening to rob him of his senses.

Zet didn't notice his master's reaction. He took his hands from his mouth and wiggled two fingers like a person's legs running. "Gone," Zet said.

It was the first word Gabe had heard from Zet's lips and sounded more like a cough, but the word had been clear enough and pulled Gabe out of his fear. "That was you making that noise? Those awful noises came from you?"

Zet nodded, then held his arms up and stomped around in circles, again putting his hands to his mouth and making those rumbling noises. He had been imitating some other minion's call, Gabe realized. *Did my minion trick the intruders into fleeing in terror?* It was the only conclusion that made sense.

Gabe felt a faint breeze of fresh air. He ran down the long hall to the entrance and bounded up the steps, peeking his head out. Save for the chirping of a few birds, the field was empty. He moved to close the double doors and noticed a dent in one of them. He thought back to the initial bang on the door and wondered why the intruders had not continued breaking down the doors. Had they used some magic to unbolt the door? Then it occurred to him: when he'd returned from testing his concoction, he had forgotten to pull the camouflage *and* lock the doors. He cursed himself. *What's the point of having a lock and camouflage if I don't use them?* He closed the doors and slid the bolt in place, pulling the string to camouflage the entrance.

"Show me. Show me what you did." Gabe demanded, walking back down the hallway. "I want you to recreate everything." Gabe ignored the acrid stench of urine hanging in the air. He watched as Zet, just out of view from the hallway, threw Clack softly against the wall, then smiled at Clack's theatrics, his dramatic reach towards Gabe, and subsequent collapse. He watched Zet's shadow dance on the wall. Whatever horror Zet was representing, the intruders had bought into it. Gabe clapped, dumbfounded, and eyed his three minions. "Who came up with this plan?"

Zet moaned while Clack propped himself against the wall and pointed toward the zombie. Moffet sat up on her haunches, scraping at the air with a tiny claw toward Zet before burying her head in her body to clean herself.

My limping, cursed minion executed a brilliant plan. How? Gabe remembered his own behavior during the invasion, and his smile faded, replaced by a glower. "I would've helped...," he said, "...but I was busy working on a potion." Gabe looked at Moffet, daring the minion who had been with him in the laboratory to challenge his statement, then realized he was staring down a rat busy cleaning itself. "There is a chance they will report our location to their guild," he said, a hardness tinging his voice. "If that is the case, stronger groups will come, expecting to fight the monster you pretended to be, Zet. Next time make sure they don't escape. All of you, get back to patrolling." He stepped into the laboratory and closed the door.

With a deep breath, Gabe remembered the lime resin he had been working on and moved towards the bench. He took a glass rod and fiddled with the residue in one of the smaller beakers. His hand shook, and the residue kicked up from the bottom of the glass like leaves in a violent wind. He tried to concentrate and control the tremor, but it only worsened, causing the rod to clink noisily against the glass. Gabe released the rod and stepped back, running his hands through his hair. He stared at the swirling flakes until they slowed and settled at the bottom of the glass. His hands began to tremble again as he released his hair. He grabbed the beaker and threw it against the wall. He felt the pressure against his skin as the glass shattered, but no pain. Gabe buried his face in his palms and cried.

FLYING debris and sand lashed at Zet like an overseer's whip coming down from all directions. A gust of wind spun him off balance, and he tumbled to the ground. He got back up in jerky movements and searched for some sign, some measure of direction, but he could barely see. The sandstorm had caught him out at the large cactus wall marking the edge of his patrol, halfway between the pyramid and the forest line. The dungeon was too far away to heal him effectively. If he couldn't return in time, his health would ebb to nothing, and he would risk becoming food for the patrolling sandworms. The master would be most displeased. Zet moaned in frustration, and sand filled his mouth. He turned his head and spat out the gritty paste.

From out of the brown haze, a ball hurled towards him and deployed at the last second, wings unfolding and flapping frantically. Iseret's talons reached for Zet. She almost missed him but caught one of his arms and dug into his flesh. They fought to close the space between them. She wrapped her thin legs around his waist and her wings around his body, then sunk her fangs into his neck and fed. The punishing winds subsided in her embrace, and he could feel her magic begin to heal his wounds and restore his energy. She guided Zet back to the pyramid with a shift of her weight.

Zet returned to consciousness and caught himself against the dungeon wall. The pain of Iseret's fangs piercing his neck faded quickly, and the cool air of the dungeon felt pleasant against his skin. *The dreams....*

At first, the recall of his dreams was fleeting, like glimpsing patches of earth in a shifting fog, but they grew more vivid each day, burning into his mind upon awakening from his regeneration cycle. Some dreams disturbed him, especially those with his master standing with a scowl and arms folded, his eyes burning with disappointment. Others, like the one he just had, were old memories. There were pleasant dreams, too; his favorites were when he patrolled out on the desert floor with only the sound of the wind and the evening air for company. He sometimes paused and watched the sun on the horizon, casting an orange glow into the sky, accentuating the scattered clouds above so that they glowed orange around their edges. *Had I enjoyed the view while patrolling, or had it changed in my dream?* He couldn't say, but something deep stirred in him when he came out of his regeneration cycle—a desire to feel the sand under his feet, to be away from walls and darkness.

Not that being underground was bad. The dungeon was growing and changing around him. He was mesmerized by the energy pulsing beneath its surface like spider webs. Often, he would stand still, mumbling and tracing the veins on the walls with a finger. Moffet would stop and chatter at him angrily until he snapped out of whatever he was doing and started patrolling again.

Zet limped the rest of the distance to the sharp turn at the end of the hall. He braced his pivot with a hand on the wall just as he had done a thousand times before and felt the warmth and imperfections of the membrane with his fingertips. As he pushed away from the wall, he felt a surge of energy suffusing his body. The pain in his leg subsided, and an amber imprint pulsed where his hand had been.

He paused at the bottom of the steps, feeling his master's presence on the other side of the entrance. The familiar fumbling of the lock and opening of the doors was accompanied by moonlight casting down on the stone at an oblique angle. The master had not looked well of late. He would periodically emerge from the laboratory, gaunt and pale, as if stricken by an affliction, and march out of the dungeon, stepping around Moffet, Clack, or Zet with an annoyed gesture if they happened to be in his way. If he returned quickly, it was generally with a curse and a scowl at anything that moved. Other times he wouldn't come back for days, and when he did, he would stumble down the hallway and into his laboratory, mumbling and slurring his speech. Zet had not seen him for two days and could tell from the fumbling of the lock that he would be different.

His master stepped down and wobbled at each step. When he reached the bottom, he looked at Zet and squinted as if he could barely make out the face before him. "You try making the bloody firelime resin!" He sneered and stumbled down the hallway.

Zet broke away from his patrol when his master was quiet for an extended period. He found the master passed out on one of the tables. Zet couldn't tell if the pungent smell was from the vomit pooling next to the master's table on the floor or the various concoctions on the other table. He took the keys from the master and walked back up to the dungeon entrance, and closed and locked the door. When he returned to the laboratory, he put the key back in the master's pocket and stepped away.

While walking back through the doorway to patrol, he felt a tingle. *Did the master command me to make the resin?* He had said the words, but something about the interaction didn't seem right, as if his master had given the order to someone who was not there. *But I was there.* He felt his eyelids grow heavy, and he slumped against the threshold, his vision fading.

"GET THE BLOODY RESIN, MINION," the apothecary demanded in a thick accent, spittle forming on the corners of his mouth. "Take the flasks to transport, or do I need to call for the scourge?"

Zet felt his hand reach out and grab one of the flasks from the wooden holdings.

"What is it?" Zet asked.

Leonid's eyes went big. "Wha...what did you say?"

Zet leaned forward. "I asked you what is in this flask."

The apothecary turned red and puffed out his chest.

"No," Zet said, "you will answer my question or cease to exist."

The apothecary's mouth worked wordlessly, then he deflated and broke eye contact. He pointed to the flask in Zet's hand. "This is firelime resin," he said. "A flammable liquid often used against heavily-protected enemies like soldiers covered in metal or carapaced creatures in the outlands. When used properly, the enemy will cook in their armor."

"Show me how to make it."

"I don't think I can teach you that. There are trade secrets involved, and you're a minion."

Zet felt the heat in his face, and his other hand came up and made a fist. "I wasn't asking," he said.

The apothecary gulped. "I see." He turned to the table. "You need these ingredients first." He showed Zet several items on the table, explaining each of their functions, then put on his goggles and fired up the burner.

Zet came to, his hands twitching out in front of him. He

was still in the doorway to the laboratory. He walked to the table. Individual jars of calcium carbonate, ignis regia, Labularia Majus, and lime sat to one side. Zet looked over at his master, snoring softly on the other side of the table. His master was wise to prepare this challenge for him. As he began to work, a hum emanated from the energy core on the other side of the room. Zet didn't notice. He was lost in his work.

CHAPTER THIRTEEN

"What the hell was that?" Ian asked. He dipped the cloth in a bucket of water and wiped his face. Elendr stood on the other side of his desk, arms folded.

"Captain, certain sacrifices had to be made to find our destination. It is unfortunate that he died the way he did...."

"Elendr," Ian interrupted, "the man exploded on my ship. In front of my crew. You couldn't have picked a better way if you'd wanted to incite a mutiny."

"My sincerest apologies, Captain. Please, let me explain what happened."

"Enlighten me. How does one explode?"

"Aerish, Captain. His name was Aerish. What I tell you now must not be repeated."

The Mage Guild and their bloody secrecy. Ian thought to scoff at the mandate but held his tongue and continued to wipe himself down with the towel.

"Before we arrived on the boat, a ritual was performed to join Aerish's essence with an object that we could track with some precision, although to what extent remains to be seen.

This object was passed to someone heading to the island we seek." Elendr's voice dropped to a whisper. "It took tremendous power to destroy that object and kill Aerish."

"This conversation is not reassuring me, Elendr. We are heading to this island to capture this power, are we not?"

"The joining weakened Aerish considerably, and even then, it was hard to kill him. The other four mages on the ship are at their full strength. Do not concern yourself with our part. It is the village that we wish you to subdue."

"You've lost your navigator, Elendr," Ian said. He pulled a bit of Aerish from his leg and flicked it into the bucket to emphasize his point. "Where will we go from here?"

A series of muffled shouts could be heard from outside. Ian looked past Elendr at the door, alarmed.

"I believe your answer awaits you," Elendr said with a smile.

"You can get your ass up to what's left of the crow's nest and start scrubbing or go over the side of the boat—your choice," Beetle said with his hands on his hips.

Finch froze under Beetle's withering gaze and quickly glanced at the mages who continued chanting in a circle.

He's actually considering going overboard.

Barely past his twentieth summer, Finch could have passed for fifteen with his wiry frame and tousled hair. His build made him the perfect climber, and the Captain wisely took him on as a rigger. All that being said, Beetle had no compunction about throwing him over the side of the boat. That didn't mean he'd let the boy drown, but a good swim could help determine one's priorities. He was about to haul Finch up by the scruff of the neck when something flickered at his periphery.

There was a collective gasp. The mages rushed to the port side. An island had appeared; on one side, a mountain jutted into the clouds, thick with black rock and vegetation.

"Land!" Beetle bellowed.

Multiple shouts went out across the boat a split second after his yell.

"Get the Captain," Beetle ordered Finch with a swift kick, jolting the young lad out of astonishment. Beetle glanced at the silent mages standing in a row, looking up at the mountain. Without Elendr there to field his questions, Beetle was tempted to march over and ask them what sort of sorcery makes an island appear out of nowhere, but he had been briefed by the Captain of this very possibility and told to mind his own business. Instead, he barked orders to turn the ship.

THEY ARE HERE, Dai'akan.

Masima took the message from Pa'vil as Talia peered up at him questioningly. She was looking better, he thought—more alert, with some color returning to her face.

"Pa'vil has accepted Kol'val into his embrace. It was an honorable death," Masima said. He thought of touching her hand, of offering an embrace, but a display of affection felt wrong. She put her hand to her mouth and turned away.

I have killed one of them, Dai'akan, but they seek to disrupt the veil. Its fabric is woven deep in me—so much pain.

Masima heard a scream and darted back to the mausoleum. He found Pa'vil shaking on the stone with foam at his mouth. The light of his eyes flickered.

I cannot hold against them. They see all. I need blood.

I would see our enemy, Masima replied.

He walked out to the caldera's edge and scrambled to the

lip, leaving his god and daughter to their pain. His feet kept slipping off the side as he walked around the caldera, but he was careful to stay low and keep his hands gripped on the rock. When he reached the other side, he squatted down like a frog with strong gusts threatening to push him back into the pool of otai. There it was, a sizeable vessel in the distance with bright white sails deployed, tacking toward the island. Pa'vil was right. The enemy was here. Masima searched for other boats but saw nothing.

How long would it take them to reach the island and climb the mountain?

Masima did the calculation in his head and decided the time was right. He would make a deal with Pa'vil, and if it worked, his grandchild would have a chance at survival.

"We should scout the best place to make landfall, Captain," Elendr said. "The mages tell me the islanders know we are here. Waiting until night would only give them an advantage."

They veered north and circled the island counter-clockwise. In stark contrast to the southeast portion of the island, where the mountain plunged into the ocean at steep angles, the other side opened up into fertile, mostly flat land. The entire northern portion was felled, with large swaths sectored into crops. He used his monocular to call out the various exotic fruits he recognized growing out of the ground and from the trees. Even as anxious as his men were, they were sick of salted beef, fish, biscuits, and beans, echoing Ian's excitement at the prospect of eating fresh food. There was no such reaction from Elendr and the mages, who stood at the bow. The mages kept their gazes fixed at the top of the mountain.

As the Stork skirted the island's western edge, Ian spied a

beach with several small canoes hoisted onto logs and some visible building structures more inland. He searched again but did not see a soul. They continued southward to a lagoon at the base of the mountain.

Elendr turned from the bow and approached Ian while the mages stayed, moving their heads in quick jerks as if they were wolves picking up a scent.

"We land there," Elendr said, pointing to the lagoon. "The mages tell me that the source of the island's power lies at the top of that mountain, Captain. You will find the villagers somewhere north where we saw those buildings."

"We are to advance on the village and capture them, then?" Ian asked.

"You were hired for your ample experience, Captain. I leave it to you and your men on how you wish to handle yourselves," Elendr said.

Ian collapsed the monocular and put it in his pocket before pulling his cutlass from its sheath. He slashed it through the air several times in a flourish before sheathing it in one smooth motion. "I think we can handle ourselves. What do you say, men? Are you ready to earn your gold?"

"Aye!" Came the reply as multiple crewmembers shoved their fists into the air.

Elendr grinned at the show.

"Good luck, Captain, to you and your men. We will meet you back here. Two days as we agreed. Per our contract, you can return to the mainland if we do not come down. I would advise taking the villagers to the Guild representative with whom you spoke earlier."

When they had anchored off the island, Ian turned to Elendr. "What do you plan on doing with them?" he asked.

"The villagers?" Elendr looked to the mages and paused

before answering. "They will be reeducated and start a new life serving the Guild."

Ian could not keep the doubt from his face. He had displaced people once before while in the military. Half were put to the blade for insolence, while the remainder were useless, reduced to a stupor after losing everything they had known.

"I care for my boat and my men, Elendr. I doubt the villagers will come with us without the mages, and I will have enough concern as it is with all of us returning in one piece if this doesn't go as planned."

"The mages will return, and the villagers will know and accept their situation. I would not waste my time worrying about that which you cannot control. Do your job, Captain."

While the crew was transported using the ship's pram, Elendr rowed the mages separately on the ship's dinghy. Leonid and Finch stayed back to care for the Stork.

"I'd pay to get one of them to take off that hood of theirs," Beetle whispered to Ian as he shifted from side to side, watching the mages disembark with a wary eye.

While standing on the island, Ian deployed several men to secure the area and ordered others back to the ship for supplies.

"Two days, Captain," Elendr reminded him as he and the mages departed for the mountain.

"You have my word, Elendr. We will wait the two days."

"Where are their provisions? Their weapons?" Beetle asked when they were out of earshot.

Ian hadn't noticed, but Beetle was right. The only visible container was a small satchel strapped across Elendr's back.

"Perhaps they carry something beneath their robes." Ian doubted the words as he spoke them.

~

THE COOL AIR of mid-morning had evaporated into a mugginess by midday, and Ian's neck and arms itched. He wore a plain linen shirt and breeches, his bloody jacket abandoned and draped over a wooden chair in his quarters. There had been no time to clean it properly. He knelt and passed his hand through the placid waters of the lagoon, frowning.

"You worry about the mages?" Beetle asked, standing off to one side.

"They know what they're about," Ian replied. He stood up and bounced a smooth stone in his hand. Two scouts had been sent north to where the buildings had been spotted. Samson traveled the beaten path the mages had taken in the opposite direction up the mountain while Quinton skirted the beach. The crew busied themselves, setting up camp and mapping the island.

"Two days is a long time to wait, Captain. It wouldn't be the worst thing in the world to capture some villagers and head home."

"Without waiting, you mean?"

Beetle shrugged. "Now that you say it, Captain, don't sound so bad. Get in. Do the job. Get out."

"The job is the contract, Beetle. I won't be running away before we've fulfilled our part. Besides, do you think escaping the mages would be so easy? You may wake up in your bed one day, fat and happy with a wife and children, and find one of those mages standing over you. The last face you'd ever see. In the meantime, you'd have to think about when it was coming. Do you want to live the rest of your days like that?"

"Wife and children? That don't sound like me, Captain. I prefer the company of harlots and cutthroats."

"So you are fond of saying, but the point is the same,

Beetle. From what little we've seen, crossing them may be as good as slitting your throat."

"Well, we wouldn't want to leave a job undone, would we?"

Covered in sweat and wide-eyed, Quinton broke their conversation when he ran into camp. He had served with Ian in the military as a scout and was a hard man, so when Ian saw the scared expression on Quinton's face, he pulled him out of earshot from the other men.

"At first, nothing seemed out of the ordinary," Quinton recalled. He had been careful on approach, weaving in and out of the dense jungle as he made his way along the beach. When he saw the buildings, he crawled deeper into the jungle and advanced slowly until he spotted the villagers.

"They were all just sitting there waiting in a field," Quinton said, his thin fingers trembling. "A hundred and fifty maybe, mostly elderly, with spears and bows. I watched them a while before this old lady stood up in their midst and looked right at me. Captain, I'm no braggart, but there ain't a person alive who could've spotted me from that distance, but she looked right at me like the trees between us didn't exist."

"What did she do?" Ian asked.

"She spoke." Quinton shook his head in disbelief. "There's no way I could've heard her speak, Captain. Maybe if she had yelled, but when she spoke...it was as if she were standing as close to me as you are now."

"Did she say what she wanted?"

Quinton looked up from fumbling with his hands. "You, Captain. She wants the leader of our group to speak with her. Consider this an invitation, she said."

Ian weighed Quinton's words carefully. *Elendr didn't mention anything about the villagers having this power. And over a hundred? That's way too many to take back. What are we walking into?*

"Grab a drink, Quinton."

"That sounds like a fine idea, Captain." Quinton turned to go before Ian caught his arm.

"I don't have to say it, Quinton, but...."

"My lips are sealed, Captain."

He had always liked Quinton, a military man to the core.

Samson came not long after, his aged face haunted, much like Quinton's had. His jowls shook with his hands as he relayed how he came upon the villagers, how an old lady had stood and pointed at him with her staff and commanded him to meet with his leader. Ian dismissed Samson like he had Quinton, with a promise to secrecy. But in many ways, the damage had been done. His men knew something was wrong.

"I don't much care for our options," Ian said, relaying to Beetle what the scouts had seen. "The jungle is too thick and wet to traverse, and the beach and path are too narrow, ripe for an ambush," Ian said. "They have the advantage no matter how it plays out. And it appears from the report of both scouts that they're waiting for us, for me. Perhaps I should have asked one of the mages to stay behind to counsel us?"

"Captain, the men are nervous, but I think they'd rather fight by your side than near the mages."

"I'm going for a walk, Beetle."

"Where to?"

"Into the lion's den. You're in charge until I get back." *If I come back.*

CHAPTER FOURTEEN

"You're drinking too much," Miranda said.

"Did you hear what I said?" Gabe collapsed onto the chair nearest the window, happy to be off his feet. He had been standing too long in Marlowe's Tavern off the Central Square, nursing one beer after another until his last coin was spent. "The minion made the resin."

Miranda sighed. "Blaming the minion for a bad mixture? That's a new one. Wish we could've used that in school."

Gabe's face darkened. "I'm telling the truth."

"Listen, Gabe. You've been drinking these last weeks plenty. Please don't shake your head at me. Colin told me so."

"He should try working instead of spying and tattling," Gabe mumbled.

Miranda ignored his comment. "I haven't sent a message to the Guild or walked down to the tavern and confronted you. Why?"

Gabe was tempted to point out that she was too sick to walk down to the tavern, but he recognized the rhetorical nature of the question and kept his mouth shut.

"Because you've got a lot to worry about. I recognize that you are trying to survive and that our financial situation is dire, but I have my limits. I can't see you self-destruct like this. You tried to do this in school and when Mom and Dad died. You and alcohol don't work well together. Wait. Let me finish, and then you can have your say."

Gabe shut his mouth. He felt small and vulnerable in front of her. Seeing his sister angry pulled him out of the comfortable buzz of inebriation.

"Your nerves are frayed, and the beer calms you and allows you to continue, then you drink more to have the same effect. Before you know it, your sleep is plagued with nightmares, and when you are awake, you're drinking to get back to where you were when you first started to fall apart. This is a downward spiral that has almost gotten you twice. Except for this time, we don't have our parents or the benevolence of the schoolmaster to bail you out. It's just us." Miranda coughed before continuing, "As to the resin, maybe you got lucky making it in a drunken haze and don't remember. Or maybe it dropped from one of those adventurers that attacked you, and your minion dragged it in. I don't know, but we don't have much time. The resin is due soon, and you've already been attacked once. Also, Colin told me that multiple dungeons in the area were destroyed. No one is taking credit, and no memory crystals were generated. The Scavenger Guild is happy, but the other guilds are not. You are wasting precious time and resources. It's dangerous out there. The dungeon needs to be stronger. You need to be stronger. I can't lose you. Not like this. I need you to fight." Miranda went into a series of racking coughs, her body shaking violently.

Gabe sat down, and his voice dropped to a whisper when Miranda had finished coughing. "You're right. I've been drinking too much. I'm sorry. The drinking stops now." He looked away from her, staring at a painting of a galleon on the tide at sunset. It had been their mother's favorite.

"But I didn't imagine this," he said. "I woke up, and the resin was on the table, and the minion thanked me for the challenge of making the bloody thing. Miranda, the minion who could barely muster a groan, can now speak in complete sentences. His voice is still rough, but I can understand him. I took the resin in my hand and examined it in light. It was as green as an emerald and smelled of equal parts ammonia and lime. Textbook. I went outside and tested the potion. You know what happened?"

Miranda shook her head.

"The tree went up in flames faster than a guild tax going into effect. I almost burned the damn forest down. I was lucky the ground was wet. The thing is, Miranda, I couldn't have made resin that potent on my best day. Zet is the only other creature capable of such a thing, and it's taking the work and thanking me for the trouble. Is a minion going to lie to its master?"

"But, Gabe, it's a minion. Why would it...how could it make a potion?"

"I told you. It said I had ordered it to make firelime resin and then something about learning how to do it during regeneration. I don't know what it meant by that," Gabe said, running his hand through his hair. "I don't think I want to know. By the Empress's grace, it could barely stand when I first brought it to the dungeon. Now, it's walking around speaking and making potions."

"Potions? I thought we were talking about a potion."

Gabe dropped his head, then peered up at Miranda. "Do you know how much a potent resin like that would be worth on the open market? The Empress herself would pay top dollar. Mom and Dad used to make potions like that."

"What'd you do?"

"I saw an out and took it. I ordered it to make a whole batch. I've got a day left before Professor Galdon's order is due. I know it isn't right, but I'm desperate. As you said, my nerves are shot. If I even look at a beaker, my hands begin to shake. I can't stop thinking about the intruders coming to kill me. My life was forfeit, and the minion saved me. And now it's making my potions. What will I do?"

They sat silently for a while, then Miranda spoke, "If what you say is true, then it upends everything we know about minions. Maybe you could talk with one of our old teachers or someone in your guild. Make a hypothetical and see what they say?"

Gabe shook his head. "They'd revoke my diploma or dungeon privileges if I even hinted a minion could do this work. I can't trust anyone, even fellow guild members and former teachers. Only you. What should I do in the meantime? I don't want to go back to the dungeon."

"No, Gabe." Miranda sat up, her lips pursed. "You have it all wrong. This is a gift. You get your butt back to that dungeon and learn everything you can from that minion. Your life and mine depend on it."

Gabe's face went pale white, and he felt a weight drop in his stomach.

"Don't you see? This is an opportunity to learn," she said.

"Oh no," Gabe said in a strained whisper, "the dungeon is under attack."

MOFFET CAME RUNNING into the laboratory and squeaked at Zet in alarm. There were people outside the dungeon. Zet put the half-made resin to one side and turned off the burner. Next to him, several columns of flasks full of firelime resin sat in a wooden crate. Zet enjoyed making the potions and working with his hands. He sensed his master far off in the distance. Whoever was out there was not friendly. A loud banging sound echoed down the hallways from the entrance as if to confirm his suspicions. Clack came up behind Moffet and rattled its jaw in a warning. They both looked to Zet, waiting for orders. Zet slumped over the table and went into a regeneration cycle.

"REMEMBER, it's important to visualize each stroke before you carve it into the dungeon's skin. The dungeon's life force will often spill out and cover your work. Unless you memorize the strokes, you will lose your way, rendering the incantation impotent...or wrong. Ah, something to eat." The woman turned away from her student and faced Zet as he held up a tray.

"Tea and crackers," Zet said.

Mara's eyes brightened. "Did you hear that, Warren? The zombie speaks. Where does Aatma find them?" She laughed. She leaned over and took a cracker from the tray. "Hmm, a bit of honey in that. Perfect. Just put the tray over there," she gestured to a nearby desk with a candle, ink, and papers.

Zet complied. He bent down and examined the symbols on the papers. They looked like the writings on some of the walls throughout Aatma's pyramid.

"What are these?" he asked.

Mara turned from her work, "Why are you speaking to us, minion? Know your place," she scoffed.

Zet stepped forward, "because my master's dungeon is being attacked, and his survival lies in these writings. These symbols bring the dungeon to life, do they not?"

Mara and Warren nodded as one. "This is Haqi, the ancient language of magic. It is dangerous and forbidden for all save members of the guilds. Even then, I cannot teach outside my guild without special permission."

"Teach me Haqi," Zet commanded.

Mara started to speak, then hesitated, her face contorting then relaxing. "Very well. Haqi tells the otai, the liquid carrying the energy, how to flow." She went over to the desk and picked up a paper. "You see these symbols? Each is made up of individual elements. If you know the elements, you can get a sense of each symbol's meaning. Knowing the symbols and grammar of Haqi allows you to build more complex and powerful incantations. Most guilds teach snippets of Haqi, enough of the writing, speech, or gestures to cast a simple spell to suit a member's needs. Even mages, who specialize in Haqi and use it to change their surroundings and bodies, only know a fraction of the language."

"There are different components to the language, then? How do they work together?"

"As much of the language was lost before the time of the Ancients, there are whole sections of my guild dedicated to answering your question. Haqi's components are intricately linked. The language has no letters, so each symbol must be memorized with a sound. There are at least ten tones that we know of, which must be pronounced correctly, or you risk changing the meaning and how the otai flows, a potentially deadly mistake. The accompanying hand gestures to the spoken word can change depending on what elements are in the symbols. The potency of the language is amplified if you can combine the components. Theoretically, a person who could harness the dance between speaking, gesticulating, and writing could be very powerful. This is why access to the language is so restricted. The speech is muted, and the gestures and writings on dungeon skin are blurred out when memories are captured for consumption by the masses. My guild members may study the language, but we cannot use it. And what we discover must be passed off to closed councils and ultimately the Empress herself for approval of its dissemination and potential further study."

"You mention the writings on dungeon skin. How does the dungeon know Haqi?" Zet asked.

"That is a strange question, minion," Warren said. "It is the otai that yields to the language of Haqi, not the dungeon."

"Silence," Mara said. "I am the teacher, and you are the student, Warren. Know your place. I will teach him."

Warren apologized and took a step back.

"The dungeon is a much larger organism than a human, with a higher capacity for otai. The energy core acts to store and circulate the otai, controlling its potency. In turn, the otai flows in accordance with the Haqi to bring incantations to life.

"Otai is the paint, Haqi is the instructions, the dungeon skin is the canvas, and I am the artist. I understand. Teach me how Haqi serves the dungeon master," Zet said.

Mara nodded her approval at Zet's metaphor and gave him a blank paper. "Let us begin with the elements. Copy them onto this sheet, but write small and lightly as papyrus and ink are in short supply."

Zet focused on the sheets on the desk, and the stack deepened. The inkwell on the desk tripled in size and filled to the brim. "I will begin by writing large elements and write as much as I need to," Zet said, sitting at the desk.

"As you wish," Mara replied.

~

THE METAL BOLT snapped with a loud clang, and the door to the entrance splintered and caved in under Kryle's war hammer. He dropped his weapon, bent down, and pulled at the remainder of the door, ripping it from its hinges.

Lena moved up next to him and peered down into the dungeon. Her dark hair framed a stern, freckled face. She searched for any sign of life. "The dungeon looks young. Many of the energy lines appear underdeveloped," she gestured to one side of the wall. "This should be entertaining. I think the masses will approve of multiple viewpoints. Activate your memory crystals." They pressed their fingers to their temples as one and spoke the familiar phrase of Haqi, activating the memory crystals in their pockets.

Camden opened his hand, and a sphere of light appeared. He pushed it forward with a languid movement, and the sphere continued down the steps and hung in mid-air several paces in front of Lena.

"The Jade clan is ready for blood," Kryle said. Tattoos covered his neck and one side of his face.

Lena tried hard not to roll her eyes. Her partners had a way of turning on the theatrics when they knew people would relive their memories. "Stay alert. We didn't get this far by taking chances." Lena knocked an arrow in her bow and descended the stairs sideways as the light source continued ahead of her at a fixed distance." She got down to the bottom of the stairs and looked around before whistling with her hand. Kryle and Camden made their way through the entrance and waited. "I don't see any Haqi on the walls and no obvious mechanical traps. The entrance is secured. Kryle, take a look down that side," Lena said, gesturing to the right with two fingers.

Kryle pulled up to the edge, his back against the warm wall, and turned his head slightly to take a peek.

Camden made a flicking gesture. The ball of light shot around the corner and down the length of the hallway.

With the ball's light, Kryle glimpsed a rat scurrying away from him and a man at the far end carving into the wall. The ball hit a barrier and dissipated, sending blue lines of light dancing across the air.

He pulled back and relayed to Lena and Camden what he had seen.

Lena walked over to where Kryle stood and stepped into the hallway, pulling the bowstring taut. She aimed just above the outline of a man's head at the far end and let the arrow fly. It whizzed down the long hallway in the blink of an eye and ricocheted off the same invisible wall the ball of light had dissipated into. The man at the end of the hallway didn't even look at her when she fired the arrow. *He is either incredibly dangerous...or stupid.* Lena swung back around and felt the heat rise in her face.

"He has a weighted shield protecting him."

"We should look down the other side," Camden said, still standing at the bottom of the stairs.

"Good idea," Lena replied.

Camden walked over and stepped into the hallway, not bothering to find cover. He pulled a dark object from his pocket.

"I hope you're casting a protection spell with whatever you have there. You are an open target."

Camden raised the object. "Beef jerky," he said as he took a bite and chewed.

"How can you eat at a time like this?" Lena hissed. She knew Camden was posturing for a potential audience. What better way to gain a reputation than to have a snack in the face of imminent danger?

"Battle makes me hungry. Besides, the guy has a rat

protecting his hallways and is carving Haqi on the wall while we invade. Props to getting the weighted shield up in time, but this is a joke, Lena." Camden moved to walk down the hallway after taking another bite of his beef jerky.

"Don't even think about it. An empty hallway screams trap. You are taking unnecessary risks and putting the team in peril."

Camden stopped in his tracks and looked at her for a long moment. "Fine." He stepped towards her, out of view from the long passageway. "Your move," he said, "but I will put in a formal request to edit that part out of our memory crystals."

She ignored his last comment. "Cast two balls of light and send them down both hallways at a walking pace. I want both of you to follow me down the right side." Lena moved next to Kryle and waited for Camden. The beef jerky disappeared into his robes. He did as Lena asked, sending a glowing orb down each of the long hallways. Lena walked a few paces behind one of the orbs, crouching low, an arrow knocked into her bow, ready to fire at the slightest movement. Kryle and Camden followed.

But nothing attacked them. They emerged into another room with an open door in the center of the opposite wall. In front of the door was a long table on its side, with the surface facing them. Lena spied the man she had seen writing on the wall walking back and forth in a laboratory with a rat following him and what appeared to be a skeleton helping him mix potions at a table.

Camden glimpsed a rack of firelime resin potions and whistled. When he got no reply, he glanced over at Lena and Kryle. "What is it?" he asked.

"When have you ever walked to a dungeon laboratory unchallenged? Something isn't right," Lena said.

Kryle nodded and hefted his war hammer. "Agreed. Let's smash everything."

"Let's not. That's several gold marks in resin alone." Camden took out his beef jerky and took another bite, and shrugged. "Maybe that's his thing."

"What do you mean?" Lena asked

"Unsettle your opponents and scare them into leaving."

Lena and Kryle visibly bristled at the word 'scare,' but Camden spoke before they could retort, "I think he's coming out to meet us."

The man emerged from the laboratory with a slight limp, wiping his hands on an apron tied around his waist, and stood behind the desk. He had thick black hair and skin that glowed an off-yellow.

"Are you the owner of this fine establishment?" Camden asked.

"No. I work here."

"What's your name?"

"Zet."

"Can we speak to the dungeon master?"

"He isn't here."

"Typical," Camden said.

Lena frowned. "Are you going to take the fall for a boss who isn't even here to protect his dungeon?"

"He's away on business." He momentarily looked off into the distance, focusing on some unseen trajectory. "He is on his way."

Lena looked over at Camden and Kryle. They both nodded at her in silent agreement.

"Walk out, and we'll let you live."

"I can't leave," Zet said.

"Suit yourself," Lena said as she knocked an arrow. "We don't leave survivors, and that desk isn't going to protect you."

She fired the arrow, which ricocheted off the shield again, breaking in two and tumbling to the floor.

"The desk isn't for that," Zet said.

Lena was about to ask what the table was for, but Camden spoke first. "The weight shield will fail if we jump through it together," he said, examining the Haqi on the walls.

Lena strapped her bow and held her hands to Kryle and Camden on either side. Kryle clutched his war hammer tight with his free hand. Camden flicked his wrist, and a dagger appeared in his other hand.

"You will feel the wrath of the Jade clan," Kryle growled.

Lena, Kryle, and Camden joined hands. They jumped as one, crashing through the weighted barrier. The look of triumph on their faces turned to horror as they fell through the floor, swallowed by a blackness, then emerged from blackness in the ceiling, only to fall through the floor again. The world flew by more and more rapidly until it all blurred. The three intruders screamed in unison until the hole in the floor closed. They slammed into the floor with an explosive force, sending blood, metal fragments, and wood in all directions. The laboratory remained clean, protected by the upended table.

Zet turned and walked back into the laboratory to continue his work.

CHAPTER FIFTEEN

K neeling next to Pa'vil, Masima recalled a journal entry by the Dai'akan Koti, who had lived centuries past. *When you speak to Pa'vil, say no more than you must, for if you give him an opening, he will break from his interminable despair and tear you apart.*

My life for my grandchild. That is my offer. Masima sent the thought and waited.

What game are you playing? Your life is not enough. I have spent what little energy I had to crush that spirit weapon.

There is another with me—my daughter.

More blood, yes. Bring her, and I will feed. With two, the island may yet have a chance.

My daughter and my life for my grandchild. That is the deal I offer.

Your grandchild is not worth saving, a pebble on the shore, no more.

Then we die. Masima held his breath.

What would you have me do with a child?

Pa'vil had not discarded the idea. Masima exhaled.

Deliver it far from here, away from the island. Safe. Protect my grandchild before you take your freedom.

Pa'vil's hand shot up lightning-fast and grabbed Masima by the throat.

I am not your plaything, Dai'akan. I am your god.

The thought bellowed across his consciousness. He squinted in pain and clawed at the hand, struggling to break free, but Pa'vil's grip was like iron. Masima had miscalculated badly.

Forgive me. Forgive me.

Masima fought back against the blackness crawling into his periphery.

My life and my daughter's for the grandchild. You need not care for the child. Merely deliver it to safety. Please. Then you will be free. If you kill me, my daughter will not come.

Masima held onto the last thought, letting it slip beyond the horizon and into the abyss before he lost consciousness.

In Ian's mind, he had given himself a one-in-two chance of being shot on sight. So, when he walked out of the thick foliage, he was surprised to find a field full of people who largely ignored him. Instead, they sat in thick grass, eating fruits and talking like an invasion into their island was an everyday occurrence. He was regarded with a few curious stares before a man the size of a boulder, covered in tattoos, stood up from the crowd and walked over to greet him.

"Follow," he said, guiding Ian to a stone bench near the village where an old woman leaned heavily on her staff. Her white hair framed a face full of wrinkles, and her eyes sparkled with intelligence.

"I am Ioane," she said. "Some would call me a leader, but

many refer to me as 'mother.'" She smiled and placed a hand over her heart in greeting.

Ian had never seen a complete set of teeth in someone so old. "I am Captain Ian Ryall of the Stork." He mimicked her gesture.

"Please, sit with me, Captain," she said.

Ian obliged her, tucking his feet under the bench and folding his arms beneath his chest. "Please, call me Ian."

"Rangi, you may leave us."

Ian gave a slight nod to Rangi, who returned the nod and walked back into the field.

"I thought this a trap," Ian said bluntly.

Ioane frowned, "There would be no honor in that."

"Why invite me into your midst? I now have an accurate count of your people and your capabilities."

"Pa'vil, in his infinite wisdom, has allowed us to understand that what was once forbidden must be weighed and judged when a new path is set before us. It is my responsibility, my burden, to hear and understand your words. I am the vessel by which Pa'vil decides and sends us down the true path."

"Who is Pa'vil?"

Ioane's eyes went wide at Ian's question. "He is the one who provides. He touches your life even if you know him by a different name."

Ian hesitated, waiting for Ioane to elaborate. But when she said nothing, he asked, "Did you know I would come alone to speak with you as I have done?"

"I did not. But I reached out to your men peacefully, and they left without raising arms. I hoped you would be a competent leader and accept my invitation."

"My scouts tell me you spotted them in a manner most peculiar, that you knew where they were when no one could have known." Ian studied Ioane. "How?"

"Over these hundreds of years, Pa'vil has blessed me with the ability to stretch my senses, to listen, feel, and taste what others could not. When you hear a palm tree sway in the wind, you hear creaking and rustling, yes?"

"Yes," he managed. *Hundreds of years!* He had met a magistrate who had made it to 92 years old. Blind and feeble, he was carried about by his grandson like a babe.

"Instead, I hear the wind's fury, the trunk's indignation, and the tree's roots as they strain in the soil."

"That sounds overwhelming."

"I have had several of your lifetimes to acclimate. Let me ask you a question, Captain. We have shielded ourselves from the outside world since Pa'vil shaped us from his flesh, yet you have found us. The men that traveled with you, the ones that climb the mountain as we speak, how did they do it?"

There was an eeriness in the calm surrounding Ioane. Her eyes seemed to burn into him. "They had a tracker, some beacon that pointed the way. I do not know how it was done. They are a secretive bunch, Ioane. They are mages and seek the power that lies at the top of your mountain."

"And you believe there is good to be had on this path?"

"I do not care," Ian answered honestly. "I need money. That is why my men and I are here."

Ioane laughed and touched his knee. "Thank you for your honesty. I see your purpose. The true battle will not be waged down here but up there." She pointed to the top of the mountain. "We will not interfere in their quest simply because we cannot. We may yet follow you on your ship and in our canoes without raising a finger in resistance."

Ian turned to her. "You would abandon this island? And come of your own free will."

"If Pa'vil wishes it. We will. But if he decides to fight and calls upon us, we will all fight."

Ian watched the villagers in the field, eating and conversing. This was not a people worried about a battle. They had abdicated their choice to whomever this Pa'vil was. Ian felt the hairs on his neck stand. "I wish to avoid bloodshed, Ioane. Do you think your god would come willingly?"

"I cannot know Pa'vil's wish. The only one of our tribe who might know that answer is up there with him. Go back to your people, Ian. The decision will be made shortly. One way or another, you and I will meet again."

THE WARMTH of a hand on his. Physical touch.

Give me the blood in your veins, and I will forgive you.

"Father," a voice said.

The world ebbed and flowed into focus. Masima opened his eyes and groaned. He felt like someone had scraped the inside of his throat with a hot rake. The soft light from his staff and dagger hurt. He rolled onto his side and coughed violently, then felt his pulse. It was light and rapid. He was alive. There was movement at his feet. Talia came into view, searching his face, concerned. A rustling came from somewhere above, and Talia looked up, then tensed with eyes wide.

"Help me up, my child," he said hoarsely.

Dai'akan, do not leave me to die. Do not abandon your god.

Masima ignored Pa'vil and staggered out of the mausoleum with Talia supporting him under one arm.

They are coming, Dai'akan. Would you seal our destruction? I let you live.

The cool air greeted Masima, and he turned to see the sun sinking in the western sky.

"Forgive me, Dai'akan. I waited and called. There was no answer. I feared for your life and entered without permission."

"You made the right choice," Masima said. He thought of the deal he had almost struck. His blood was too valuable for Pa'vil to kill him.

"Kol'val gave his life's blood to Pa'vil. It was an honorable death. I saw his body." Talia began to cry.

"Shhh, little one." Masima had called her that as a child. He put his hand on her shoulder. "Listen carefully. Pa'vil is being hunted. They are his enemies, and they are like him. They climb Mount Laiya as we speak. We must give blood to Pa'vil to give him the strength to fight. Do you think you could do that?"

Talia looked scared but nodded. "I don't understand. Are you saying the others are gods like Pa'vil?"

"Don't worry about that. Can you give your blood to Pa'vil as Kol'val has done?"

"If my god commands, so will I do."

"Yes, good, stay at the entrance to the caldera. If you see or hear someone approaching, come in and tell me. Understood?"

"Yes, Dai'akan."

Masima went back inside. He kept his distance from Pa'vil, collecting his dagger and staff. *Your enemies are closing in, Pa'vil. Time is running short.*

Feed me, Dai'akan, and I will meet them with open arms.

My life and that of my daughter for my grandchild. That is the price for your freedom.

Pa'vil's hand twitched. *I should have squeezed the life out of you when I had the chance. You are worthless.*

My daughter and I will leave you to your ruin.

And yours. They will harvest you—a fitting justice for abandoning your god.

We will take our chances.

BETRAYER!

Masima felt his hands shaking with a mixture of fear and anger.

Goodbye, Pa'vil.

WAIT. Your life and your daughter's for the child? I accept your offer.

He thought of Talia as a child, playing with the other children, laughing, and throwing sticks with Palani. *My Talia. May her unborn child protect her from Pa'vil.* He felt the soul dagger pressing against his leg. It felt heavy. He held the rod out before Pa'vil, and his god gripped it. The air shimmered around Masima as Pa'vil repeated the oath. He felt the words' veracity and knew Pa'vil was bound by his promise.

Talia walked in, breathing heavily. "They come, Dai'akan."

"How much time do we have?"

"There was the cracking of a rock and a shout. It sounded distant."

"Close your eyes, Talia." He did not wait to see if she followed his command. He walked to the other side of the stone slab, dragged Kol'val's body to a dark corner, and dropped him. There was no need for Talia to see his corpse again. It would only distract her. "Open your eyes and turn towards me. Kneel where I was as best you can and do as I do."

Hurry, Dai'akan, they come. Pa'vil's urgency dripped through with the thought.

"Listen well, Talia. I will cut Pa'vil's hand then yours. Hold your hand to his and give him some of your strength. There will be a sharp pain as Pa'vil enters your body and takes your blood. When you feel that, focus on Pa'vil's prayer, say it in your head, and then rip your arm away when you feel your heart beating hard. There will be a wound, but you will heal quickly. I will be asleep. Don't worry about me."

The lie stung. There was no sleep, only death, but he did want her more distracted. Masima could have laughed at that moment. For so long, he had kept this all secret, followed the path of the Dai'akan faithfully. But for the second time in a day, he was doing that which was forbidden, letting Pa'vil feed from another. He looked at his daughter and saw the tears streaming down her face as she clenched her teeth and wore a determined frown over Pa'vil's desiccated body. *So brave, my beautiful Talia.*

"Look at me."

She turned, and her large, brown eyes locked onto his. Her face was rounder with the pregnancy, but she was still beautiful, just like her mother. He could not remember the last time he'd held her gaze.

"Help Pa'vil as best you can; he will protect you."

"I do not understand what is happening, but I will do as you say, Father."

She had called him father. He would've admonished her severely for saying that not a week past. He smiled at her, "You are a good daughter and will be a good mother."

Feed me, you fool. They are almost upon us.

Masima leaned the staff against Pa'vil's stone bed, so that its light stood equidistant between Talia and him, illuminating both sides. There was a slight line on Pa'vil's hand from when he fed from Kol'val. Masima traced the cut on that hand and then cut the other. Pa'vil groaned with the pain. He then cut their hands and passed the dagger to Talia. "Tuck this in your waistband and embrace Pa'vil's hand with your own."

May you conquer our foes, Pa'vil, and earn your freedom.

Masima bit down hard on his tongue and tasted blood with the familiar pain. He would not cry out his last time.

His vision started to blur as his pulse quickened, and he felt woozy. "Now, Talia. Pull away." The words felt thick and unwieldy.

A high-pitched, piercing scream told him she had followed

his commands. He did not have the strength to respond. He wanted to comfort and tell her he was sorry for all that had happened and what would happen. His senses faded, and the world turned black again.

I've got you, Dai'akan. Your last thought will be of my victory over you.

My last thought will be of my grandchild floating happily in my daughter's belly.

What? She is still pregnant! Oh, you know not what you have done!

Masima slumped to the ground. Pa'vil's rage chased him into death but found no purchase.

CHAPTER SIXTEEN

G abe woke in the shadows, beams of light filtering through the canopy of leaves overhead. He mentally checked his body, flexing and moving his limbs. Nothing appeared broken. He reached out and felt the dungeon at the edge of his consciousness. It was still, and creatures were moving about, but he was too far away to distinguish who they were. If they were the intruders he sensed at Miranda's apartment, why was his dungeon still running? *How am I still alive?* He stood slowly, wiped his mouth, and then the detritus from his clothes.

He remembered getting through the city gates and breaking into a run, trying to reach the intruders before they destroyed the energy core. His legs had failed mid-stride, and he'd tumbled to the ground, branches clawing at him. He reached up and traced the scratches crisscrossing his face. *What would've been my plan if I'd reached the dungeon?* It was all so fuzzy, but he was pretty sure he'd never worked that part out.

It was midmorning when Gabe arrived at the entrance. The

entrance doors were strewn about the ground, obliterated. He entered the dungeon and looked down both hallways. His eyes confirmed what he had already felt. They were empty. He walked down the left hallway, then came around the corner slowly. He had sensed a weight on the other side of the room, so he wasn't startled when he saw the three bodies piled to one side, stripped of armor and weapons. But the grotesque image gave him pause, and he took a step back into the shadows of the hallway. He had seen dead minions before, even dissected a few in anatomy class, but he had never seen a dead human.

"Master," he heard a voice say at the same time the door to the laboratory creaked open. "Welcome home."

Gabe took a deep breath and stepped back out into the room. "Yes, I have returned." He tried to think of something else to say, but his mind moved slowly. "I see you have almost disposed of our intruders," Gabe gestured to the bodies without looking at them. "How did you beat them?"

"I cast a weighted shield followed by a nested portal," Zet said, gesturing to the symbols on the walls, ceiling, and floor. His voice rang out in the silence, deep and clear. "They were not difficult to kill."

Gabe remembered seeing a demonstration of a weighted shield in school. They were easy to cast but required written Haqi and large amounts of energy to block anything meaningful. Gabe had never heard of a nested portal.

"When did you learn Haqi?"

"Before the attack, during my regeneration cycle."

"I don't understand. How could you learn it so quickly?"

"Not all of it," Zet said. "Only what I needed to deal with the invaders."

"But how...why..." Gabe searched for a question but shut his mouth. There was no point in arguing that a bumblebee was too fat to fly when one was flying in front of your face. "How did you know how strong to make the shield?" He asked.

"From Moffet's report on their vibrations, I extrapolated how much they weighed. The austere setting of the dungeon and the weighted shield provided a distraction from the portal incantation on the ceiling and floor. When they jumped through the shield, the portals activated, and they fell straight into the floor portal, which fed into the ceiling portal. The floor portal was set for one-hundred pass-throughs before closing. They died on impact. I put a desk between us to minimize the splatter of blood and material into the laboratory."

Gabe tried to follow Zet's explanation, but the bodies in his periphery distracted him along with something about Zet's manner. He felt a twisting of his insides, and his breathing quickened. He reached out to the energy core.

"I am disappointed in you, Zet. Our energy core is nearly depleted."

Zet's shoulders slumped. "You are right, Master. With my limited capacity, I could not find a way to reduce energy expenditure. A recursive call in Haqi can be expensive. I will try to avoid them in the future."

What was he talking about? Gabe examined Zet for the first time in weeks and realized what had made him uneasy. Zet's once mottled and sickly face was smooth with barely a hint of yellow. The sparse hair on his head had become a thick, black mop. And his eyes burned with that same intelligence he had only seen in spurts when Zet had first been transported. His zombie looked better than he did.

"Do not worry," Zet continued, "I have finished the potions with Clack's help. After fulfilling this contract and selling the Jade clan's materials and your remaining stock, you will have enough to summon an energy healer to refill the core. I also found these," Zet reached out and opened his hand. Three memory crystals glittered on his palm. "The residuals could be lucrative but may attract unwanted attention."

"What do you mean?"

"The incantations I used may be restricted. What would you have me do?"

Clack, Zet, and Moffet all looked at Gabriel, and his brain ground to a halt. He peeked into the laboratory with a furtive glance and felt a sudden dread as if he were suffocating. Then he spotted the box of resins. "Um, sell the crystals to the Information Guild, and bring me the box of resins. I will deliver them to Professor Galdon personally."

Zet returned to the laboratory and reappeared with a wooden box full of glass flasks, each filled to the same height with a viscous liquid that glowed a soft green. "Master, we can use the transport circle if you wish."

"I am aware, minion. Dispose of the bodies as soon as possible."

Zet nodded and handed the box over.

"During your regeneration cycles, can you learn how to make medicines?"

Zet closed his eyes momentarily, leaning against the wall, then opened them. "Yes, I can learn medicines."

Gabe felt like he might cry. He needed to ask this question but stuttered, struggling to get the words out. "My sister...she's dying from consumption. Can you heal her?"

"I don't know," Zet said.

Why doesn't he know? Couldn't he just close his eyes and find out? Gabe tried to think through the questions he needed to ask. Sweat stung his eyes, and supporting the weight of the box in his arms felt untenable.

"Do what you can to save her."

"As you command, Master. Bring her here, and I will do my best."

"You are a limited creature and would be much more valuable to me if you could travel." Gabe turned and walked down the long hallway and out of his dungeon with the box of firelime resin.

COLIN WAS FINISHING a stench potion at his workstation when he heard the explosion coming from the direction of the entrance. The dungeon's skin brightened with the increased speed of otai running through its veins. There were screams, and the beast master came running through with a pack of flesh hounds on his heels. Their sharp teeth gnashed at the air, and saliva stained the floor in their wake.

"A bit odd, that," Suzanna said behind him. She, too, was watching the oversized dogs race down the passageway. "They usually wait to release the hounds unless the intruders are deep in the dungeon. I've only ever seen it happen once." Suzanna's long hair was grayer than blonde, and she walked with a gait favoring the right hip. She had been an apothecary at the dungeon for years.

Colin stayed quiet and watched the dungeon master enter the room. He could tell from her furtive glances and frown that she was worried. Her overseer stood beside her, and they looked to be having a heated exchange in hurried whispers. Colin couldn't make any of it out.

All the apothecaries at all the tables turned their heads, watching the interaction. The overseer threw up his hands and stalked away, marching deeper into the dungeon.

Colin turned to Suzanna for a possible explanation.

"I think he's going to release the drakes," she said.

"The drakes?" Colin had only seen them released for meals and training, never for a battle. "Without the beast master?"

Another explosion echoed through the caves, this one much closer. Everyone around Colin jumped at the loud noise. Some people ducked under the tables, while others sprinted to where the overseer had gone deeper into the system of caves. The dungeon master stood to the side, her hands clutching her hair and fear plastered across her face, looking lost.

Colin approached her with a few others and peppered her with questions. "Who is attacking? Is it one of the top clans?" He watched as the dungeon master shook her head emphatically. "Then what is it?" Another explosion sounded. This time, in the cave next to them. "What's coming?"

The dungeon master looked down at him. "A single creature," she said. "I don't know what it is, but it has destroyed everything we've thrown at it."

Colin turned and followed his fellow apothecaries away from the explosions, running to the energy core. As he ducked down a passageway into the next cave, a giant creature leaped over him and screeched. Two more drakes followed, passing over him and soaring into the cave he had just left. He got up, and the dungeon master hissed behind him, "Keep moving, you idiot."

Sapphire strolled into the large room full of benches and workstations. She spread her wings and heard the familiar pops of cartilage. They felt good.

A fat man with a scourge yelled out from the opposite side of the cave. He lifted his hands and brought them down in a quick motion. Three sleek drakes dropped from the ceiling and advanced on her, two on her flanks and one in front, their narrow heads bobbing up and down as they walked.

Sapphire spoke Haqi while making a series of hand

gestures. A lightning bolt surged from her fingertip and struck the overseer in the chest, sending him crashing into the wall.

The drakes screeched and pounced on her simultaneously. Silent through the air, their claws extended. Sapphire raised a hand and mumbled an incantation. She opened her fist, and the air expanded suddenly. The drakes flew backward and skated across the ground, tearing into the dungeon's skin with their claws to catch themselves. She reached her hands out as if gripping their heads from a distance, uttered another incantation, then twisted her hands. Their heads were ripped from their bodies, and they fell into a growing pool of their own blood.

When she stepped into the last cave, she heard the cries and pleas from a group of people hunkered in the far corner. The energy core with its thick tendrils sprouting into the wall was behind them. They looked like insects trapped in a spider web. Sapphire purred at the pain emanating as they begged for their lives. That was what Sapphire liked most about humans; their threshold for pain was so low, and if you listened close enough to their torment, it sounded like a symphony.

She walked across the cavern, avoiding an obvious pit trap in the center. She saw a thin woman to one side slump in resignation when she avoided the trap and knew her to be the dungeon master.

"You," she said, pointing at her, "step forward."

The dungeon master did as commanded, trembling terribly.

"Gabriel Shook. Do you know of him?" she asked.

The woman looked confused, "I do not."

Sapphire raised her hand, disappointed yet again, and began an incantation.

"I know him," another voice said from the crowd.

Sapphire watched the small man emerge. She stopped the

incantation and lowered her hand. "Where can I find him?" she asked.

"I don't know, but I can lead you to someone who will know."

"And who might that be?"

"His sister," the little man replied.

Sapphire smiled. "You will be spared," she said.

"That is all I ask," the man said, stepping away from the crowd and moving to her side.

"Now, where was I?" she raised her hand and began speaking Haqi.

GABRIEL KNEW something was off with the Professor when he arrived. The man constantly fidgeted, pushing his spectacles up on his nose and glancing about, expecting monsters to jump from the shadows. He was happy to see Gabriel's work and marveled at the consistency of the potions, but he was also wary, talking about strange noises at night in the city.

"Multiple dungeons have been wiped out without anyone taking credit," he said, "and there have been several murders in the streets, including guild members. Strangest of all, just as many well-established dungeons were razed as new ones. The guilds have launched an investigation, but everyone is on edge. You must be careful." He sent Gabe on his way with a bag of coins and a worried look.

When Gabe walked out of the gates of his alma mater, he passed The Majestic, a tavern with the sign of a crown over the door. He had frequented the establishment as a student. He'd drink with his friends to relieve the stress after exams or mind surf on memory crystals to study how different dungeons operated. That was before the weight of his parents' death and his sister's sickness, before his dungeon.

"New memories just come in," a boy shouted from the front of the tavern. "Come experience the downfall of the Kinsmen Clan or relive the destruction of the Great Aatma. We've got memories to fit your every dungeon fantasy!"

Gabe stopped in front of the tavern. He thought back to his conversation with Zet in the dungeon. How little he understood. *Zet is the dungeon master, and I am the minion.* But it was far worse than that. Gabe could not fight, and the thought of working in the laboratory made him queasy. *I'm not even a minion. I'm just a burden.* Miranda had tried to cheer him up and get him to see it as a blessing, but Gabe knew that no matter how much he learned from Zet, he would never be as good a dungeon master. He wished he had never gone to the consignment shop and had been killed during the first attack.

He stumbled into the tavern and was nursing his third Winter Ale at the bar when he asked for stationery and ink.

"This is a tavern," the bartender said with a growl.

Gabe placed several silver marks on the countertop. "I need to send a message to someone in the city."

The coins disappeared, and the bartender grinned. "Looks like we are breaking into a new business." He stuck his fingers in his mouth and gave a sharp whistle. A skinny girl came running up to him. "Fetch some stationery supplies, so this gentleman here can write a message. You are to deliver it directly when he's done." The girl nodded and bolted out the entrance.

Gabe wrote quickly, unburdened by sobriety. On the back of the paper, he drew a map with directions from the city to his dungeon. He then put it in an envelope and put his sister's name on it along with her address.

~

MIRANDA WAS SITTING at her desk reading a book on flower anatomy when a knock came at the door. An envelope appeared underneath, and she heard footsteps receding down the stairs.

She braced herself on the armchair and slowly rose. She found that if she went too fast, she would get dizzy and start coughing, then need to rest longer than if she had just taken it slow in the first place.

Her brother's handwriting was on the envelope. Miranda got a sinking feeling in the pit of her stomach. She opened the letter and read:

> My dearest Miranda,
> Clarity is a beast, especially when you have been living a lie. I thought I could do this, be a dungeon master, but it's clear that I'm in over my head. I think about my feeble attempts to make a potion or the intruders that have been killed trying to invade my dungeon. Their bodies were thrown aside like pieces of meat, Miranda. It was just awful to look at. I can't continue like this. My inadequacies haunt my every waking moment. I can't go back. Please understand that I need to get away from all this. I believe Zet can cure you. He is learning faster than I ever could. Go to him. He is expecting you. On the back of this letter is a map. I'm counting on you to help him keep the dungeon and me alive while I follow a different path.
>
> I'm sorry I couldn't keep my promise.
> GS

Miranda felt the breath escape her body. She had no idea he was in so much pain. *My poor Gabe.* She knew what it was to be a burden, to feel like you were taking up space and resources but not adding anything to the world around you, to be alone in that suffering. She doubled over and wept for her brother, then shuddered violently with the subsequent coughs and wheezes.

Time passed as she lay on the floor, recovering from her exhaustion. Gabe had left her to his minion, she realized. *Am I to rest my hope on my brother's delusions?* She did not know, but she had only half-believed Gabe when he described what his minion was doing. *Maybe Zet can help me find my brother?* She had to get to the dungeon and figure out where he had gone. She wiped away her tears and studied the map he had left her. The dungeon wasn't too far from the city gates. With a heave, she used her rocking chair to stand up and crossed the room to get her coat. She folded the map into her pocket, then opened the door, leaning against the threshold and coughing into her elbow. When she stopped, she stepped through and saw Colin coming up the steps. He looked just as surprised as she felt seeing him.

"Colin, what are you doing here? Shouldn't you be working?"

"Ah...I should be, but there was a bit of an accident. The dungeon is shut down. What about you? I'm surprised to see you out of the apartment. Do you need something? I can get it and come back. You really shouldn't be out in your condition."

Miranda felt her energy dropping, standing at the doorway. "Colin, that is very nice of you, but...," Her eyes lingered on him, and she noticed Colin was sweating profusely and had dark circles under his eyes. *Something is wrong.* The revelation came to her with such certainty that she felt adrenaline rush through her body. "Okay," she said weakly and fished inside her purse. She brought out a silver mark and went to hand it to him. "If you wouldn't mind picking up two tomatoes, three cups of rice, and some dried figs, I could make a meal for us."

Colin waved the money away. "It's my pleasure, Miranda. Go back inside and rest. I'll be back before you can take your coat off." He stood there, watching her wide-eyed, waiting for her to turn around.

Miranda obliged, putting her hand on the threshold and pivoting back into her apartment.

"I'll be right back," he yelled out as soon as her back was to him, and then she heard him race down the stairs and slam the entrance door.

If I don't go now, I'll never go.

Miranda stepped back out into the hallway and shut her apartment door. She had to get to Gabriel's dungeon.

CHAPTER SEVENTEEN

Like a jellyfish wrapping its tentacles around her flesh, electric fire coursed up Talia's arm. Her father's instructions had evaporated, replaced by a torrent of pain. One long scream filled her ears, but she could not identify its source. She tried to keep the prayer to Pa'vil in her mind, but the pain drowned out her attempts. Finally, she heard her father's voice in the distance, telling her to pull away. Talia pulled her arm downward and wrenched it sideways with all her might. Her hand separated from Pa'vil's, and she felt a spray of warm blood across her face. Talia came crashing back into her senses, and the pain receded to a dull ache traveling up and down her arm. She lost her balance and collapsed against the wall. The wind was knocked out of her. Slick with sweat, she took large gulps of air and cried, clutching her hand to her chest. She was sure it was ruined, but the only mark was an oozing gash on her palm.

Talia was dimly aware of movement from above, the ebb and flow of light. She lifted her head and saw a figure swinging a stick, the Dai'akan's staff, up and down on the other side of the stone slab. The rhythmic sound of wood striking flesh came into focus. The figure stopped and turned towards her, leaning against the stone. It was Pa'vil, her god. His chest rose and fell rapidly in the gloomy light. Where there had been dry flesh anchored by sinew and muscle, there was now skin, half-formed. His face twisted with rage when his gray eyes made contact with hers. He growled and took a step back, grabbed the glowing orb at the top of the staff, and crushed it with a grunt, plunging them into near darkness with only the light of her father's dagger in her waistband illuminating the small space.

A shiver coursed through Talia's bones. She had been dimly aware of another movement within her and realized the baby was kicking. Talia put her hand on her stomach and breathed, trying to calm herself.

A noise came from outside, the crunch of feet on crushed rock, followed by a stone hitting the water.

The enemy comes. "Protect me. Pa'vil, tell me what to do!" She cried in panic. There was no answer. She felt as if she were back in her bed as a girl, pleading for Pa'vil to hear her, to tell her why her father had to leave the family to serve him.

My father. He was somewhere on the other side of the slab. He would know what to do. Scooting along the wall, Talia moved away from the entrance and quickly came up against the back wall. She slumped into the corner, confused and exhausted, trying to think. Something cold and soft was next to her. She pulled her hand away. More footsteps sounded from outside. "Pa'vil, what do I do? Please answer me," she said.

Two lights, blue and pointed, flashed in the dark. A dizziness gripped Talia. She felt like she was in freefall and placed each arm against a wall, bracing herself.

What is happening to me?

Breathe easy, child.

And there it was, a thought that was not her own. She knew it to be Pa'vil's answer.

I am going mad. Instead of the idea floating in her consciousness, she could move it, like sliding parchment back and forth on smooth wood. She pushed the thought until it disappeared. It was gone. What had she been thinking?

You do not know what madness is, child. Look into my eyes. You are speaking with your god as your father did before you. Pa'vil took a step towards her, his eyes brightening, then stopped. *It is too late. Your father played his hand well, even if he did not fully understand his actions. What's done is done.*

I do not understand.

You do not have to understand. Only obey. He has bought the life of your baby. You are the new Dai'akan. It should not be so, but you are tied to me as your father was before you. The enemy comes. I will lay down on the slab once more and feign helplessness. Remain still. Keep your face hidden. Cover the dagger. Do not move. Do not speak. You are useless to me if you are dead.

As Pa'vil says, I do.

This was madness. Instead of pushing her idea towards Pa'vil, she pulled it towards herself and kept it close. She knew it would no longer be hers if it slipped beyond that edge.

Pa'vil's eyes dimmed, and fingernails scraping against rock told her he was climbing back to his resting place.

Another light skirted across the entrance. There were no voices, only the shuffling of feet. Talia remembered Pa'vil's instructions and looked down, her hair covering her face. She bunched up the side of her skirt and placed it over the glowing hilt of the dagger, plunging the small space around her into darkness. Several figures stepped through the entrance, their silhouettes outlined by the outside light, and into the mausoleum.

Talia's baby kicked hard. She feared the invaders would hear her breathing.

Four is too many, even if I were at full strength.

A chanting started as Talia received Pa'vil's thought. Four what? People? What would they do to him? *Dare I ask a question of my god?*

What would you have me do?

Already they begin. They will seal me in magic and take me with them. The island will die without me. You can do nothing.

The light brightened as the chant rose in pitch. Talia felt the connection to Pa'vil wane. She thought about what Pa'vil had said, that the island would die without him. She had to do something for her god, for her unborn child. Slowly, her hand reached under her skirt. The chanting grew louder. Talia's fingers inched up and grasped the hilt. She pulled it out, and a scraping sound of metal against stone caused her to tense as she tucked it under her legs. Talia held her breath. There was a shuffling of feet.

"So, you live, little one. Look at me," a voice said. Talia did not move, and a hand grabbed her hair and yanked her up. She stared into the glowing eyes of a pale man with swirls of red tattoos dancing on his skin. She gasped.

A man or demon?

"Playing dead?" he asked. Talia saw three figures behind him, and Pa'vil thrashed about on the slab.

"I could use a snack," the man said. "It looks like there has already been a feeding frenzy here." He grabbed her arm and yanked it up from underneath her. He froze at the sight of the gash on her hand and hissed.

A fire burned through her. These were the enemy of her god and people. Talia felt the baby kick again. She thought of her unborn child, Kol'val, and her father's sacrifice. The fire blossomed and spread from her chest and out to her arms. She brought her other arm up in a quick, side-ways motion. The man sensed the movement and moved his head back, but she moved with a speed that shocked her, and the dagger plunged into the side of his neck. There was a sound as if water had been thrown on embers. The creature gurgled, blood spilling from his wound. The red swirls slowed and froze on his face as the light of the dagger pulsed brighter. Talia pushed him back-ward. He fell onto his back, his arms and legs curled towards his body.

The chanting stopped, and the others looked at her as if she were an insect that needed crushing. She screamed and stepped back as they moved toward her. She did not bother reaching for the dagger in the man's neck. He was too far. She knew she would die, knew that it was over for her and her unborn baby.

I have failed you, Pa'vil. Forgive me.

Talia pressed her back against the wall and covered her stomach with her arms. She heard the shuffling of cloth as they raised their arms. There was a popping sound in her ears. She closed her eyes, ready for death. It did not come. Talia opened her eyes in confusion and saw the creatures raining blows down on her at an impossible speed, but they did not hit her. Something was blocking their attempts, some shield. They stopped in unison.

One reached back with his hands, his mouth open, clutching at his back, and then fell. Pa'vil stood behind him with the dagger and muttered an incantation, moving his hands in the accompanying Haqi gesture. The air around the mages and Talia thickened, slowing their movements to a crawl. He followed the mage down, shoving his other hand into the middle of his back. The mage convulsed as Pa'vil took his blood. The partially fresh skin crawled across the rest of his face. His physical strength returned, and he gave the mages a vicious grin as they turned to face him in slow motion.

Pa'vil spoke Haqi and punched his hand toward the figure nearest him. The mage flew back and slammed against the wall. He struggled against an unseen force pressing against him. There was a muffled scream and then a crunch. The mage tumbled to the floor. The other mage crossed his arms and spoke.

Pa'vil dropped to the ground as a rush of energy passed over him. He grabbed Talia and pulled her with a violent jerk. She rolled onto her side and felt a deep rumble. The air thinned, and the night air rushed in to greet her. She sat up, and the walls of the building were gone. Talia looked back at Pa'vil, who sat in a crouch, his engorged arm throbbing with the blood he had taken from the man lying beneath him. His eyes shone a rich violet.

Stay here, he commanded.

Pa'vil broke from his position and leaped into the air, impossibly high. A loud splash a moment later sounded his landing, followed by a series of grunts and a scream. Talia tried to follow the movements from the glow of their eyes, but they moved so fast.

Come with me. Pa'vil limped in and offered her a hand.

What of my father and husband?

They are dead. They sacrificed themselves to give you this chance.

Talia suddenly felt nauseous.

We must go.

Leave me. I am not worth your time, great god. Protect our island.

Pa'vil threw back his head and laughed. *Your father told you nothing. A true Dai'akan to the end.*

He picked her up and carried her in his arms as if she

weighed nothing. He raced across the land bridge to the caldera's edge. A single figure rose to stop them.

"I am Elendr," the figure said, "I have feasted on the otai and will avenge my masters." There was a dull gleam in his eye.

As if drinking my piss would make this fool a full mage.

Talia did not understand his message. Pa'vil tilted his head, and a wall of air marched out in front of them, accelerating as it went. Elendr stood his ground with a sword grasped in both hands before him. The air hit its mark and wrapped around him, carrying him outward. Talia saw his mouth open in a silent scream. She thought he would fall away when the air pushed him out of the caldera, but he kept traveling outward and disappeared into the darkness.

A groan escaped Talia's lips as she felt a tightening in her pelvis. Pa'vil frowned, then pivoted. He began chanting, and the lake began to churn and slosh. A dark mass rose from the caldera with a tendril between it and the lake, twisting like a snake. A ball of otai rippled above them. Pa'vil walked to the caldera's edge with Talia firmly in his arms. He looked out at the stars. Tears streamed down his cheeks.

How I have missed the world.

Pa'vil looked at her, and his expression changed a dozen times in a second. Thoughts, jumbled together, flooded her mind. *You are not Kyra. Your father tricked me. You should not be here. The world is at risk. Did they kill my Kyra?*

Talia was about to ask what he meant when Pa'vil lurched forward off the path and onto the steep slope. They moved down the mountainside, picking up speed, weaving between dark shapes. She turned away, looking over his shoulder to see the giant sphere of otai following just above them, glowing in the darkness. Talia closed her eyes and buried her face in the crook of her god's neck.

~

A CRASH OUTSIDE brought Ian out of his dreams. He heard the shouts of several men, jumped up from his cot, and pulled on his belt and sword. He walked out of his tent and grabbed a torch. "What happened?" he yelled.

Beetle emerged from the foliage, wiping himself down. "Captain, it appears Elendr has had a bit of a fall. He's still alive, but not for much longer. Our scout reports he dropped from the sky."

Ian rolled his eyes. "I wish I could say I was surprised. Show me," he said.

"Make way for the Captain," Beetle shouted. The men parted, and Ian followed Beetle into the thick foliage. They didn't need to walk far before coming across Elendr splayed out on the ground. Judging by the angles of his body, his back was broken. Elendr looked up at the sky, his eyes searching. He sputtered and coughed up blood. Ian knelt beside him.

"I've seen men run through with a sword in better shape than you, Elendr. What happened?"

Elendr looked pale, but there was a slight glow to his eyes.

"Mages are dead," Elendr whispered. "Miscalculated. Go, Captain."

Ian stood up and held his torch out toward the village. He looked around in the darkness.

"Miscalculated? Elendr, a man exploded on my boat, your mages were all killed, and now I find you falling from the sky? A miscalculation implies that some calculation was made in the first place. I don't see any evidence of that."

Elendr made a series of weak coughs, struggling to respond. "Wrong," he said.

"Elendr, is this thing that killed the mages coming down from his mountaintop to kill my men and me?"

Elendr shook his head, and then his eyes lost focus, and he looked out into nothing and rambled incoherently.

Ian circled Elendr, pulled out his sword, and thrust it into the man's heart. "An act of mercy. Soon we will be wishing for the same," he said.

A rumble came from the direction of the mountain. Ian and Beetle looked up in time to see two figures, one holding the other, and a large, iridescent sphere pass by them at high speed, heading toward the village.

"What the hell was that?" Beetle asked.

"Our signal to leave," Ian replied.

Ian heard a thunk as an arrow landed near him. Shouts rang out from the direction of the camp.

"Return to the ship," he bellowed, running for his life.

CHAPTER EIGHTEEN

Colin pounded on the door several times and began shouting Miranda's name. An older woman with a shawl wrapped around her large frame stepped out of her room down the hallway and gave him a dirty look. Colin turned to her and apologized, stating that he was worried about Miranda as she had not seemed well earlier in the day. The woman waddled over, producing a key from somewhere beneath her prodigious dress.

She moved him to one side with a gentle swat. "Miranda, honey, are you there?" she called with a knock on the door. When she didn't hear a response, she turned and looked at Colin, her eyes narrowed in suspicion. "Stay here," she said. She opened the door and called Miranda's name from the threshold, then stepped inside and shut the door behind her.

Colin heard her footsteps around the apartment as she walked from one place to another and paused, calling Miranda's name. When the door opened, she said, "Miranda isn't here."

"That's odd. She was expecting me," he said.

The woman gave him a once over, "You sure?"

"Yes, I'm sure. I brought ingredients," he said, holding up the box of food.

"I can leave her a message if you'd like."

"No, that's quite all right. I can come back later. I'll leave this at her door." He put the box down and stepped back. *Will the creature just kill me?* Colin considered going to the guild. Maybe they could offer protection. But then he remembered how Sapphire had destroyed the dungeon, and doubt crept in.

The woman shook her head and pointed behind him, "Get your head out of the clouds and mind the stairs on your way out."

He blinked and then laughed nervously. Half-turning, he grabbed the finial at the top of the stairs post and took the steps in a halting fashion. The old woman stood there, shaking her head. He thought he heard her murmur "idiot" before returning to her apartment and shutting the door.

Colin emerged onto the street and looked at the sparse evening traffic. *Where could Miranda have gone?* He couldn't understand why she would leave when she was so sick. Colin thought back to their interaction and remembered a moment of hesitation when she looked at him intensely. Colin had dismissed it as her not feeling well, but perhaps Miranda was more perceptive than he thought. Had she gone to check on her brother? Colin walked down the street, his head whipping back and forth, scanning the alleyways and building facades. His fast walk turned into a jog. He needed to find her and quickly. His life depended on it.

GABE WOKE up to the swaying of a wagon on the road in darkness with a splitting headache and a cloth stuffed in his mouth. He was on a hard surface with his hands and feet tied before him. He winced in pain. *What happened?* He had stumbled out of the tavern and watched the fireflies dance in the fading light of dusk. Then, stumbling back to his dungeon, he had seen Colin in the street and asked him how Miranda was doing, more in gest than genuine inquiry.

Even inebriated, Gabe had recognized that something was wrong. Colin had stared at him, eyes wide and mouth open as if Gabe had been a hydra, then he turned and ran away. *Then what?* A voice sounded from above him.

"They'll make a fine addition to the Empress's forces. But this one, Mikhal, is ours, bought and paid for."

The deep voice was familiar to Gabe. It had been the voice that had beckoned to him from an alleyway, asking for help. He remembered taking a few steps toward the man lying on the ground, then heard footsteps behind him. Gabe felt nauseous and realized that his hangover was not helping his situation.

"Our special guest has decided to grace us with his presence. You've been in and out of it for days. Thought we might have ruined your brain with that hit."

There was a tug at the cloth in front of Gabe, then light flooded his vision, blinding him. "Ahh," he moaned through the gag.

"Not so tough without your words, are you, dungeon keeper," a man dressed partly in leather armor and sitting on a bench on one side of the wagon said. He took a bite of an apple in his hand and chewed noisily. "Suppose his guild will want to know what's happened to him?"

"Not for a while," a thinner man with a shaved head and a red band over his right bicep replied. "They're busy figuring out who's destroying all the dungeons. Listen, you," he said, staring down at Gabe, "I'm going to pull that gag. If you start yapping in Haqi or rambling on about how powerful you are and how your guild will save you, my boot is going into your mouth instead of this rag. So, kindly keep your mouth shut unless spoken to. Do we have an understanding?"

Gabe nodded slowly, not because he had pondered the man's words and made a decision, but because his headache had worsened.

"My name is Agnon, and this is Mikhal," he gestured to the man sitting across from him, then reached down and pulled the cloth from Gabe's mouth. "You'll get to know us real well."

Gabe took a deep breath through his nose and mouth. He worked his jaw and felt the soreness from having his mouth gagged for so long, then leaned his head back against the wagon's side. He wanted to sleep, but the wagon rattled along the hardpacked road, and the sudden jolts caused his head pain to worsen.

Mikhal followed his eye line to the wagon following them full of men and cargo. He chuckled. "Those are the less fortunate souls. Not dungeon masters like yourself. They're fresh meat bound for the Empress's army up north."

"Sorry about the bruise on your head," Agnon said. "We didn't have much time, but Mikhal and I are here to protect you...."

Gabe heard a sickening *thwack* and looked over at Mikhal. An arrow was sticking out of his chest. The man tried to speak through frothing blood, then tumbled over and landed beside Gabe. A chorus of jeers went up around them. Agnon got down low and felt for Mikhal's pulse. He cursed and pulled the cloth sack back over Gabe, telling him to keep his mouth shut for the second time as chaos erupted around them.

～

WHEN SHE WALKED through the city gates, the guards and people gave Miranda a wide berth. She mumbled apologies, coughing up blood and stumbling. Her face felt hot, and her hands clammy. She struggled to recall the directions to Gabe's dungeon, then remembered to look at the map. Each step was more onerous than the last, and time slipped away as Miranda focused on the task before her.

When she came to a clearing under the moonlight, she thought all was lost and collapsed to the ground. Her dress was torn to tatters, and she was too weak to cough. She hadn't thought to bring a lantern or torch and didn't have enough light to read the map. She wanted to lie down and embrace death, tired of the fight that had robbed her of her health this past year, tired of the pain of losing her parents and Gabriel. *Had she lost Gabriel?* She couldn't remember what had happened to him. No, he was right there, right in front of her. She could see his silhouette near the trees on the other side of the field. "Gabriel?" she called out. "Is that you?" The figure waved to her.

The soft grass was inviting. All she had to do was stop struggling, relax her body, and let the eternal dream take her. But she did not want to give up in front of her brother. He would have to come and get her. *I am forever a burden.* Miranda crawled towards Gabriel, one knee and hand in front of the other. She would not be a burden.

When she reached the figure, she was surprised that it had disappeared. In its place, there were stairs leading down to an entrance. A rat sat up on its haunches, chirping at her. She crawled down the stairs and onto the soft skin of an active dungeon. The energy colors flowed beneath her hands, pulsing greens, blues, and oranges. She thought she might have hallucinated and was still at the edge of the field, slipping into that eternal dream. But she felt a hand on her and looked up to see a man she did not know. His eyes glowed a soft gold, and his brow was creased in consternation.

"Miranda." He stated.

"Yes?" she asked.

"Your brother has delivered you to me, and by the looks of it, not a moment too soon."

Miranda nodded dumbly as if it all made sense. "My brother. Where is he? Who are you?"

"I am Zet. Your brother is far away. What is important is that you are here with me."

Zet reached down, scooped Miranda into his arms, and carried her down the long hallway and into the laboratory.

CHAPTER NINETEEN

Ioane awoke in the elder's hut amid the Surge. Not even on feast day, when the villagers feasted on the pregnant coral reef worm, po'aloni, and diluted otai, had it been this strong. The ache in her bones and the tightness in her muscles that had been as familiar to her as the grooves in the pommel of her walking staff were gone, replaced by a strength she had not felt for a hundred years. Her legs vibrated with restlessness, urging her to run. *Why is this happening?* She breathed deeply and focused on its meaning. Her mind raced through possibilities at a speed she could barely track. To embrace the Surge was a precarious balance. Every few years, on the feast day, a villager would relinquish control to the warrior spirit, running into the jungle or swimming out into the open waters, never to be seen again.

Walking quickly down the stairs, she turned at the bottom and saw points of red light appearing in the field. *The eyes of the villagers—they have all entered the Surge. Pa'vil has spoken: repel the invaders.* Raising her hand to her mouth, Ioane gave out three caws, the signal to start the hunt. Ioane and the villagers gathered their weapons and stalked forward as effortlessly as shadows shifted with the light. When she stepped up to the boundary where the open field met the jungle, her people were with her, stretched out at her flanks in one long line. She looked up to the stars and then back to the jungle before her. "Pa'vil sings to us this night," she said, sweeping her head side to side. Her voice rang out against the rustling of leaves in the dying wind. "Pa'vil, guide us true." Her last words were repeated up and down the line. She took one last look at the village and then charged forward with a cry. The rich soil greeted her like a hug from an old friend. The night revealed its secrets in shades of gray, and the jungle smelled of rotting wood and healthy flora, of putrefaction and sweetness.

She ran for a time, her legs carrying her in long strides, quickly navigating the obstacles. When she heard voices in the distance, she stopped and unslung her bow, notched an arrow, pulled the bowstring to her cheek, and released the arrow. It arched upward and disappeared in its parabolic trajectory, raining down into the camp of her prey. The twang of bowstrings releasing around her followed a split second afterward. She pulled another arrow and advanced through the jungle, pausing to release arrow after arrow until there were no more. Flinging the bow behind her, she took up her spear, spinning it in her hand. The flicker of fire greeted her through the trees.

A line of sailors waited for her when she broke through the trees. One advanced towards her, a look of terror painting his face. He raised his crossbow and pulled the trigger. She felt something strike her leg. Her gait compensated for the inconvenience, but that is all it was, an inconvenience. Ducking under the sweep of his blade, she brought her spear up and thrust it into his abdomen.

"Red-eyed demon," he said with a groan and collapsed, writhing in pain.

Ioane brought the spear down hard on the side of his head with a loud crack. He went quiet. Something bit into her side. She twisted and raised her spear to meet a blade. There was a loud clash. A large body moved in, and the man whose blade she had crossed went sprawling. Rangi bellowed next to her, his red eyes smoldering in the dark. The sailors nearest them took a step back.

"Arutua!" He yelled, hoisting his spear and throwing it into the chest of a sailor who flew back several feet and lay on the ground motionless.

"Rangi," Ioane yelled. She was on the ground. Blood was all around her. She thought most of it was hers. She tossed her spear to him. He caught it and turned back as the sailors rushed in. Several villagers appeared around her.

Behind the line of fighting, Ioane saw panic. The sailors had abandoned striking camp. Some were jumping into the ocean and making a break for the Stork, while others stood watching the battle, frozen. Ioane's eyes made contact with Captain Ryall. He stood behind the line shouting, struggling to maintain order. He saw her then, a grim expression on his face. She nodded, one leader acknowledging another in the heat of battle. The gray of the night dissipated, replaced by shadows and darkness. She felt an emptiness as the Surge left her. Pain rushed into that emptiness. Her side was on fire, and she could no longer move her leg. She had fought well. Pa'vil had guided them true. As he always did.

A RUMBLE, deep and vast, woke Talia from her sleep. She moved slightly, and her head came up against a hard, sloped surface.

She was in a canoe, she realized, on the beach, looking back into the village. Another rumble sounded, stronger this time. She struggled to raise her head, to search her surroundings, then fell back. A spasm started in her abdomen. She felt the need to push, to fight.

Not yet.

Pa'vil pushed the boat from the shore and hopped in. The large sphere of otai floated behind him.

You are in the Surge. If you push, the baby will come, and you will die. You must wait.

The urge is too great.

Her abdomen spasmed. She breathed rapidly.

Pa'vil studied her and placed his hand on her stomach. Words left his mouth, but she did not recognize the language. She felt her muscles twitch and then go flaccid. She lay there, her head propped up, watching Pa'vil turn and raise both hands. He began to chant, and the otai seemed to fight against itself, giving off sparks and churning. It began to spin faster and faster. Pa'vil brought his hands down, and the sphere lowered with his hands. She felt a jolt as the sphere entered the water, and the canoe lunged forward.

Pa'vil moved his hands slightly, and Talia felt the direction of the canoe shift as the canoe turned. Mount Laiya shrank in the distance. Suddenly, one side of the mountain gave way, and a vast plume billowed out from its side. A deafening blast followed. The canoe rocked violently. Talia thought she would go over the side, but the air above her thickened, and she hit a wall as the canoe fell back into the water.

What is happening?

The mountain has done what it has wanted to do for a thousand years. My prison protects it no more. The volcano has awoken from its slumber.

Prison? Pa'vil had created Arutua and given her people life, a paradise cut and hewn from his flesh. *Why would he refer to the island as a prison?*

The smoke was spreading rapidly out from the island, approaching the canoe. Pa'vil's chanting came faster. The canoe lurched forward anew.

The magnitude of what she was witnessing hit her hard. Her home was no more. The tears came again, this time for Palani, Ioane, and the others she had not known she would grieve.

Am I all that is left?

There was no answer to her question. Talia closed her eyes and tried to block the anguish, yet the pain bit into her and wouldn't let go. *There is still my baby.*

The world had returned to its normal colors when Talia woke up. She felt like she had been beaten with a stick and left in the sun to bake.

Don't move or make a sound.

Pa'vil put his finger to his lips slowly in a shushing motion. His eyes shone brightly.

Talia thought giant insects were flying around them, but one paused before her, and she realized they were fish with wings. With large milky gray eyes, one fish buzzed closer to her and turned to the side while snapping at the air with rows of sharp teeth.

Pa'vil's chanting grew louder. The fish turned away from her and continued on its way.

One word could invite a thousand flying snappers. They would eat us alive while we screamed. We must conserve the otai.

Eat us alive. Talia did not understand how a god could die. She studied Pa'vil's face while he studied their surroundings. His cheeks were sallow, his forehead slick with sweat. He paddled slowly with an oar, grimacing as if each stroke pained him.

Talia was about to ask what she could do to help when the pain in her abdomen flared to life. She gritted her teeth and tried to stay quiet. When the pain subsided, she lifted her head out of the boat. Her neck hurt from staying bent against the boat's hull for so long. She saw movement to the right and looked into the water to see a serpent the width of their boat pass by. Pa'vil pushed her head back down into the boat.

These waters are filled with dangerous creatures. Stay still and silent.

The baby is coming.

Pa'vil gazed at her stomach with a snarl.

You will not survive the journey if you do not feed. Use your dagger to link us as you did before.

The memory of that link brought to her pain; the physical pain of him feeding on her, of the death of her father and partner, then the memory of Mount Laiya erupting in the distance and taking her mother and everyone she had ever known. Her world had been razed, with only her god and unborn child left. Tears streamed down her face. Pa'vil saw her tears and pulled the Dai'akan's dagger from the bottom of the boat, cut her hand, then his, and joined the wounds together. She did not fight him.

She expected pain, but this joining was different. There was the stab, like a worm working into her flesh, and then fluid, hot and warm, was pushed into her, pulsing through her arm and into her chest, then out to her entire body. She felt light-headed, and her body quivered in ecstasy, sharp points of pleasure rising from every pore. She convulsed and sank into the boat. It all blurred; the sky, the boat, the pleasure, her unborn child kicking. Only Pa'vil's eyes remained clear, two points of light burning like stars in a contorted face of pain. She felt herself float away from her body and move outward, beyond a threshold, and into another consciousness.

CHAPTER TWENTY

Volkmar Sashi was a rigid man with a disapproving glare for the distasteful, and he found most things distasteful. But he was the High Magister of the Haqi Guild, and his request for an audience could not be ignored, not even by Empress Inalda. The guild council had flagged a memory, and Magister Sashi stood outside the library doors waiting for Empress Inalda and her finance minister to review the crystal.

It had been delivered that morning and was nestled in a chamber etched with Haqi symbols at the base of the remembrance obelisk. Fatini sat at Inalda's side and pricked his finger with a pin as she had done. They placed their fingers in notches at the top of the thin glass form that made up the obelisk at the center of the table. It was no taller than two handspans and glowed a faint orange as the blood mixed with a reservoir of otai and traveled downward, bathing the memory crystal at the bottom. Empress Inalda and Fatini muttered the incantation of recollection and slumped in their chairs.

Moments later, their eyes popped open, and the Empress nodded slightly in Fatini's direction. He stood and went to the door. The guards stood on either side outside while Magister Sashi paced. He stopped and looked expectantly as the door opened. "The Empress will see you now," Fatini said, and Magister Sashi followed him.

"Empress Inalda, thank you for seeing me on such short notice." He kissed her hand with a bow. Inalda motioned him to sit opposite her at the table.

Fatini waited for the Magister to sit before retaking his old seat at her side.

"Magister Sashi, I am glad you are in good health. Fatini and I have just reviewed the memory. It is quite an ignominious ending to the beloved Jade clan."

"To say the least, your Majesty. It is clear that the owner," Magister Sashi took out a piece of paper and handed it to the Empress before continuing, "Mr. Gabriel Shook has had outside help. After reviewing the memory thoroughly, I wrote out the sequence of Haqi personally."

"Yes, I see it here; a recursive call from the floor to the ceiling portal lasting a hundred cycles. A clever incantation. Fatini, hand me our sheet on Mr. Shook's dungeon."

Empress Inalda reviewed the report from the Transport Guild on the dungeon's supply and quality numbers, then handed both papers to Magister Sashi.

"What is the council's conclusion and recommendation?"

"It is clear that he violated the guild precepts. A dungeon master does not have access to recursive incantations. Only the Haqi and Transport Guilds have this knowledge. We do not know how he came across this information, but we suspect the black market. The council recommends a shutdown and complete scrubbing of the dungeon, followed by a detailed inquiry."

"And what of our other problem? Has any progress been made in finding the party responsible for destroying these other dungeons? What are we up to now, Fatini?"

"Two dozen, your Majesty."

"Not yet, your Majesty," Magister Sashi glared at the papers before him. "We have our best people working on it."

"Magister Sashi, this Gabriel Shook has increased production week over week by 300%, and his potions appear to be of the highest quality. My army needs these supplies, and the council wants to shut down this dungeon and torture the one person excelling at the Great Game?"

Magister Sashi looked to Fatini as if to plead his case, but Fatini just shook his head slightly. "Well, your Majesty, torture is a strong word. But if that is what it takes...he has broken the precepts and cannot get away with this. The council was decisive on this point."

"Fatini," the Empress said, shifting her focus, "do you remember the rattails?"

Fatini grinned. "Yes, your Majesty."

"The rattails. What do rattails have to do with this?" Magister Sashi asked.

"It is a simple matter of economics, really," Fatini said. "When we installed sewage in the capital, the rats came. And with the rats, disease spread, and the people complained. The problem got so bad that we offered a copper mark for every tail. Do you know what happened?"

"The rats were decimated."

"That is what we thought would happen. But in reality, rats without tails started to appear everywhere, and rats' nests were discovered in people's homes. So, you see, Magister Sashi, an incentive is everything."

"My army is hanging by a thread, and whoever is destroying these dungeons is wiping out my supply sources. I need every potion that can be made, especially the potions that this Master Shook is providing. And what better motivator for our people than a dungeon master wiping out an elite group of adventurers with nothing more than an incantation? Hopes and dreams are created among the masses, the guilds' influence spreads, and my most promising dungeon remains operational."

"And what of the memory?"

"Blur the Haqi and release instructions on the recursive incantation to the Dungeon Master and Adventurer Guilds. Backdate some of the instructional books and memories."

"So, we are giving this memory legitimacy?"

"We are giving the people a purpose, Magister Sashi—a clear incentive. And we are serving the empire and surviving. The council would be most wise to reconsider their viewpoint. Their future may depend on it. If you will excuse me, I must attend to other important matters."

"I will return to the council with your...insights, Empress Inalda. Good day."

Fatini saw the Magister out and returned to the table. "What would you have me do, Empress?"

"Let's ensure Magister Sashi understands the weight of my recommendations and find out everything you can on this Master Shook."

"As you command."

MIRANDA LIFTED her head from the cot in the corner of the laboratory and scanned the room. A man–*no, not a man. A minion, Zet*–Miranda reminded herself, stood at the table farthest from her, peering into a vial while swirling it gently between his index finger and thumb. A rat stood beside him on its haunches, examining the same vial. The rat squeaked, and Zet passed the vial off to a half skeleton farther down the table, who continued to swirl it. Miranda blinked hard to make sure she was not hallucinating. She swung her feet over the cot's edge and tried to stand up. Immediately, the room started spinning, and she collapsed back onto the cot.

"I would not recommend standing, Ms. Shook," Zet stated from across the room without looking in her direction. "You have recently recovered from the brink of death. Your autonomic perturbations will attenuate with time, but you must convalesce."

Miranda struggled to make sense of Zet's words. She watched as he shook his head at the rat and pointed to a tiny bag at the end of the table. The rat scurried across the table, grabbed the bag, and dragged it back to him.

"I know of you," Miranda managed. "My brother told me of your brilliance in defending the dungeon. Thank you for saving his life...and mine, it seems."

"You are welcome," Zet said. He paused his work and looked up, making eye contact with her for the first time. His jet-black hair fell in curls about his head, framing high cheekbones and a strong jaw, but his eyes caught Miranda's attention. His eyes burned with a mixture of yellow and black, like molten gold stirred in with the darkest ink. She looked away, taking a moment to study the rest of the laboratory, but she felt his eyes, and her face grew warm.

She took a deep breath and felt the fullness of her chest as her lungs expanded. There was no urge to cough. Miranda remembered Zet's words: *he had said from the brink of death.* "Am I cured?" she asked.

Zet shook his head. "Technically, no. I have taken control of the energy core and joined you with it. Your lungs are heavily scarred from chronic and excessive hemoptysis, and your body is weakened due to severe deconditioning secondary to inactivity. You are drawing power from the dungeon to heal, but it will take some time. You must stay near the energy core to maintain your health."

Miranda nodded. "What does hemoptysis mean?"

"The coughing up of blood."

She stood slowly and stepped forward, bracing herself against the table. "And what does it mean to join with the core? I did not think more than one person could do that at a time. Is my broth...?" A sudden fear gripped her at the thought of Gabe's death, and her voice faltered.

"What the Guild permits and what is possible overlap but are distinct. I have performed the necessary ritual to join you with the dungeon. Your brother is alive and still joined. As your connection grows, you will sense his life force. Although his distance limits your ability to tell little more than whether or not he is alive."

"Is he in trouble? Can you do something for him?"

"I believe he is safer than if he were here. His circumstances are beyond my control."

Miranda felt distressed at the news of her brother and was about to ask about Gabe's circumstances when her legs threatened to buckle under her weight.

Zet stepped around the table and approached her. "Here, let me help you into one of the chairs." She walked across the floor with Zet holding her elbow for support and felt like she had an itch that needed scratching. When they paused next to the chair, the strange sensation went away. She described what she was feeling to Zet.

"What you are sensing is the skin of the dungeon. It is an

extension of your body now. As your neural connections adapt, those feelings will grow and change with time."

Miranda only understood half of what he said but thought she understood enough. When he eased her into a chair, she leaned back and sighed deeply, relishing in the feeling of being able to take full breaths. A hundred questions popped into her head, but she was too exhausted. She placed her hand on his, feeling the warmth of his skin against her own, and thanked him again for helping her.

"Will you be okay here?" Zet asked, concern on his face.

"Yes, if you don't mind, I will watch you work for a time."

Zet went over, pulled a basket from the bookshelf, and set it on the table before Miranda. He pulled back the cloth and revealed a loaf of bread and an assortment of meats and cheeses, then he poured her a glass of water and placed it on the table next to the basket. "Your energy usage has greatly increased. You must eat and drink as much as possible to stave off starvation and dehydration. I have constructed a bathroom for you," he gestured to a door in the far corner of the laboratory. "There are fresh clothes in there for when you wish to change."

For the next two weeks, Miranda did as Zet suggested; she ate copious amounts of food and slept through the night and most of the day. She insisted on periodically joining Clack and Moffet's patrols of the dungeon. During the second week, she climbed the steps and walked outside around the field, breathing in the fresh air and thinking about her brother. Meanwhile, her sense of what was happening in the dungeon grew stronger. She could tell when Moffet was running a circuit, or Clack was dragging itself across the floor. She could even sense Zet; sometimes, she would watch him in his work and feel his mind racing, his energy and intelligence permeating his surroundings. She desired to be next to him, to talk to him.

One morning, when Miranda was walking laps around the dungeon, she felt Zet in the laboratory. A slight tingle of frustration came from somewhere beyond her, but she knew it to be him. She walked to Zet and asked him what was wrong. He looked at her with curiosity and stated that the handle on his pestle had broken and that he needed to buy a new one.

Two days later, Miranda felt her brother, a distant presence like a mirage on the horizon. Over the subsequent days, the mirage hardened into something tangible, and she knew him to be alive, as Zet had said, although she could tell nothing more. She worried for him, but it was also an incredible time for Miranda. It was the first time in years that she was not sick, not in pain. She felt strength and endurance in her body and could walk several laps around the dungeon without difficulty. She sat and read many of the books on Gabe's shelf. Zet even recommended one, Paquette's *Forbidden Symbols of Haqi*. She had never read anything of Paquette's and was shocked at the potency of the content. She spent hours tracing the symbols with quill and paper and discussing with Zet their various permutations.

Zet was her companion, rarely stepping away from the tables. He constantly measured chemicals, mixed solutions in beakers, and taught her at each step of the process. Miranda would often join and help, and although she still didn't understand Moffet or Clack's language as Zet did, she could read their moods through her bond with the dungeon and get the gist of what they were communicating.

When Zet stepped away from the bench, it was usually to the transport circle. Shipments of basic chemicals would appear in a brilliant flash, or Gabe would send orders for noxious bombs, stimulants, sticky acids, and stink potions.

Miranda even brewed some of those under Zet's supervision. She had never seen so much money come and go, and while Zet kept much of it in the dungeon for purchases, the rest he deposited in banks through the transport circle.

By the beginning of the third week after her arrival, they had been attacked twice. Miranda was in the laboratory both times when Moffet arched her back on all fours, hissing and glaring at the entrance. Zet calmly stated, "We are about to be attacked. Miranda, please close and bolt the laboratory door."

She did as instructed, although her hands were jittery the first time. The dungeon would glow a deep crimson, and the energy would pulse faster through the walls. Miranda felt like she was in a violent storm without the winds or rain. She could sense the intruders enter the dungeon, their footsteps tearing at the skin; no pain was involved, just uncomfortable itchiness as the dungeon's skin mended.

She gasped when screams echoed down the hall, followed by silence during the first attack. Zet had shown her the nested series of traps down the hall etched in Haqi, and she didn't quite believe they would work as instructed. Then it was over. The pulses of energy slowed, and the colors brightened. Miranda no longer felt anyone walking and realized the intruders were likely dead. She looked to Zet to celebrate their survival and saw him stirring a beaker with a glass rod on the bench as if nothing unusual had occurred. By the end of the second attack, she didn't bother looking up from her work either.

On one of their walks, Miranda asked Zet why no one could challenge the dungeon. Zet smiled reassuringly, his teeth gleaming, "Their grasp of Haqi is elementary. It is like asking a child to read chemical equations. They might recognize a few symbols here or there. The best of them may even be able to write some basic equations, but they don't understand how the symbols interconnect, how the otai flows."

That night, Miranda called Zet from the entrance. He came at once and looked up at her from the bottom of the stairs.

"What is it, Miranda? What do you see?"

"Miranda held her hand out to him. Come and walk with me outside."

Zet shook his head. "There is much to do. I have several large orders to fill."

Miranda smiled at him. "They can wait. Walk with me. When was the last time you saw the stars?"

Zet heard a squeak and looked down at Moffet. The rat stood on its hind feet and pushed at his leg with two front paws. The signal was clear. He turned back and saw Miranda's heart-shaped face at the top of the stairs. She had come far from the waifish creature he had first encountered. A keen mind and strong body had emerged from the depths of that sickness, but her dark brown eyes had changed the most, sparkling with vivacity.

"These walls have been a canvas for my growing mind but also a prison these past months, painted with finger strokes and blood in equal measure. I would gladly seek a respite to be with you. Yet something buzzing deep in my body keeps my feet from wanting to move up these steps. I feel as if there is a force here," he said, stabbing at his chest, "pressing down on me."

"I know what you feel," Miranda replied. "In the depths of my sickness, I would awake at night thinking I would die, crushed by some unseen pressure. Here." She mirrored his movement and tapped her chest.

"How did you get past it?" Zet asked. His voice sounded distant in his ears.

"By focusing on the moment," she said. "Focus on what

you are doing, on your muscles as you move, on each step as you push against the stone, on the fresh air brushing against your skin."

Zet did as Miranda suggested. He felt his legs flexing as he pivoted forward and his feet crossed from the soft dungeon skin to the hard stone. When his head emerged into the night air, he felt the cool breeze but kept his head down, focusing on the steps. The pressure slowly released in his chest, and something soft gripped his hand and pulled him. Zet felt a jolt of surprise and looked into Miranda's eyes as their bodies touched. She squeezed his hand reassuringly, leaned in, and kissed him.

Zet closed his eyes and wobbled unsteadily. Miranda grasped his arms tightly, stabilizing him.

"Zet, are you okay? I'm sorry, I didn't mean to...," her voice faltered.

"I have no teacher for this," he said, opening his eyes and searching her face with alarm.

"No, I imagine you don't," Miranda said, covering her mouth and laughing. She moved her hand up and squeezed his shoulder gently. "But I don't either. Maybe we can learn together?"

THEY CALLED it the guild shuffle. At 8 pm every night, an iron bell sitting in a tower overlooking Guild Row tolled a dozen times, signaling the end of the shift. Magister Ezil had been a part of that shuffle for thirty-two years. Periodically, he would join or be joined by other high-ranking magisters as they trudged to their apartments just inside the city's northern walls. This night, wrapped in his thick, red robes, Ezil walked alone.

Light sprouted out from the center of the staff in his right hand, climbing out in both directions and enveloping the ebony stick. With his head hung low and labored breath, Ezil felt the weight of his staff in his hand. My staff, he thought with a sardonic grunt. He had taken a vow of poverty when entering the guild administration. They all had. Not even the apartment was his own, reverting to the guild upon his death or termination. But the staff was his. It pulsed a yellow light as it struck the cool cobblestone with a soft thunk in line with his slowed cadence. An energy stone no larger than a pebble sat in its center, producing all the light he would ever need. It would be buried with him in the graveyard abutting the guild, a field of energy pebbles in repose with their defunct masters.

When Ezil reached the apartment complex, a ghoul bound to the building held the entrance open. Ezil dismissed it with a wave of his hand and passed through the entrance, making his way up the narrow stairs to the second floor, tapping the energy staff to his door and mumbling an incantation. The door clicked open, and Ezil moved into the main room, closing the door behind him. He took his robe off and hung it on the coat rack before heading into his small study to collect a favorite book for his nightly ritual of reading while eating pickled herring and crackers.

"Magister Ezil," a voice said in the darkness.

The staff flared in his hands, illuminating the room. A figure sat at his desk and pulled back the cowl covering its head.

Magister Ezil could tell from her pointed ears and the discoloration of her skin—a light purple—that she was not human. He had spent his life studying the various creatures that inhabited the dungeons. "You cannot be here. The building keeper will hear of this. Minions are not allowed into rooms without permission."

"I do not belong to this building. My name is Sapphire, and I need your help." She stood up and stepped around the table. Her cloak covered her body entirely, except for the black boots sticking out the bottom.

"How did you get in here? Where is your master?" Ezil asked. He made a step towards her. The tip of his staff began to glow red as energy pulsed through it.

"You should not be so quick to threaten. I have already skinned a number of your guild members. I don't need another trophy. Tell me what I need to know, and I will disappear. You will never see me again."

Ezil hesitated. He did not know what her power source could be if she were not linked to the building. How she moved spoke of competence and raw power. *Could she have made it to the city from the outlands? Surely not. The Empress would never have allowed that.*

"What information do you seek?"

Sapphire smirked. "You are a reasonable man. I can see that. The last of your kind was not. His skin was so soft. Even flayed, it didn't lose that softness." Sapphire paused, rubbing her fingers together. "Before he died, he gave me your name. He said you would know where to find Gabriel Shook's dungeon."

"Revealing a dungeon's location is forbidden."

"Forbidden, I hear that word a lot. I find that working through pain is a good way of figuring out if something is truly forbidden. Come, Magister Ezil. Let's work together."

She stepped toward him. Magister Ezil held the staff between them. "You are an abomination. I will use all the power I have at my disposal to end you."

Sapphire reached out and placed her hand over the staff's top—the smell of burnt flesh filled the air. A loud crack came from within the staff, and they plunged into darkness. Ezil noticed only the soft glow coming from Sapphire's eyes. They brightened as she leaned forward, her nose nearly touching his. "An abomination. Yes. But not one you could hope to snuff out with your meager weapon. I'm getting bored. Let's play a game." The light of her eyes increased enough for him to see the smile on her face.

CHAPTER TWENTY-ONE

"Look at me, Nicholas," a voice said. "Son, look at me."
Tears streamed down her face. She touched them. They did not belong to her. She lifted her head. A man sat across from her. *My father, Uren, is his name.* Talia fought the memory. *No, Masima is my father.* Her vision grew blurry, then sharpened on the man's grizzled face. The wagon bounced as it hit a rut in the road.

"This is your opportunity, Nicholas. Do as the mages say and learn all that you can. They will see that you reach your potential."

She looked out the window and saw in the distance a massive white castle rise out of the hills. Talia was stunned by its enormity. Uren grabbed her chin and pulled her face back to him.

"You may be fourth born, but you carry the Landry name just the same. Do what they say and bring honor to our family."

"I will, Father," she replied, but the tears came still. She turned back to the castle, and a tinge of fear and loss crept in as if leaking from a vast reservoir through a crack in the wall. The castle blurred, and everything went white.

"Rise and come forth, Nicholas Landry."

She stood up in the pew. The heavy wool cloth covered her from head to toe, as it did everyone in the room. She went to the aisle and took measured, purposeful steps forward. Two older men stood on either side as she walked up to the dais and sat on an oversized wooden chair. She looked at the young men filling the pews, all watching her. The vaulted ceilings, painted red and black, gave the room a sense of foreboding.

One of the men approached, holding a serpent wrapped around his arm. She pulled the sleeve back and exposed her arm. That sense of fear came again. The man was talking, his voice muffled. She couldn't understand what he was saying. The colors of the room faded. Only the serpent, with its green eyes and slick yellow body, remained in focus. The snake hovered over her arm, its tongue flicking against her skin. Talia felt relief when it turned back to its master.

"The serpent has made its decision. You have shown much promise in your years here, Nicholas, and have earned the right to be called Mage. You will shed the bonds of your previous life and join our ranks. You will be known as Pa'vil, 'strong one' in the old tongue. Welcome, Pa'vil."

A thunderous WELCOME PA'VIL echoed through the pews. Talia felt pride swell in her chest.

"Down on your knees and let the rites begin," the voice commanded.

THE SMELL of burning wood filled her nostrils when she opened her eyes. A fire's dying embers sat before her. A movement to her left caused her to jump. Talia felt wary, but something else too; anticipation, lust. She was meeting someone here.

Across from the campfire, Kyra emerged at the edge of the dying light of the campfire. It was a spirit born of the outlands with translucent skin covering the glow of internal organs. Talia felt her pulse quicken. She stepped around the fire and towards Kyra.

"Nicholas, my love, come with me," Kyra said, holding out its hand.

Talia grasped it. Kyra's hand was soft, almost ethereal. They walked into the forest hand in hand. Kyra glowed a soft incandescence that brightened with the night. A chant rose from her throat, and Talia felt the air move around them. It grew warm. Talia began to undress. Kyra's hair wrapped around Talia's flesh. Their bodies touched. Kyra bit into her. Ecstasy.

TALIA LAY IN A LITTER, weak and restrained with thick rope. Four people sang in unison as they carried her up the steep path. A blanket of stars hung over her, interrupted by a steep wall of rock—a mountain. A man looked over her and smiled with a row of blackened teeth.

"What have you done with Kyra?"

"Kyra? The spirit you mated with? I do not know. Likely, it was harvested by the mages."

"No, it was my fault. Kyra did not deserve death. I deserve death. Where are we going? Where are you taking me?" she could feel the panic in her voice.

"Up Mount Laiya," Eraka said. "We have built a special place for you there."

"No, I must go save Kyra."

"You have evaded the mages and must stay with us to gain strength. We will take good care of you."

She fought against her binds. They did not budge.

"Don't waste your energy."

"Release me. I demand it. I am a mage, master of otai!"

The man laughed. "There are no masters of otai. There haven't been in a long time. Don't be angry." The man looked away from him. "Stop marching." They stopped. "We will start the process. The pain will take your mind off your troubles." Eraka took out a dagger. Its pommel glowed a soft green.

"Where did you get a soul dagger?"

Eraka smiled again, those blackened teeth looking wicked in the green light.

"The price was high, but we needed something to cut your flesh. I will be your first."

"First, what?" Pa'vil asked.

"I am Eraka, your first Dai'akan."

"I don't understand."

"There will be time for us to talk. You will understand."

She felt the dagger cutting into her palms, her blood running down her arm and off her fingertips.

"Hand me the jar," Eraka said. He pulled off the lid and took out a worm the size of an index finger. "These are blood-worms from the Owinawa Desert. They are creatures of otai and will permit you to feed directly so that we may build a reservoir and one day bring about the prophesied Children of Otai."

"Hold his hands open," Eraka commanded.

Talia fought but knew it was futile.

Eraka placed a worm in each of the freshly cut wounds in

her palms, and they burrowed down into her flesh greedily. She screamed and fled the memory.

SHE STOOD OVER A CORPSE, flogging it with the Dai'akan's staff. Anger coursed through her veins. The bag of blood had tricked her into protecting its kin. *Otai running freely through an unborn child? Oh, bag of bones, you have destroyed us all with your clever trick.* Her anger would not abate, and the staff was her instrument, rising and falling, striking the corpse. There was a movement off to her right. She paused, and her raspy breath filled the confined space, the prison she had known for an eternity. She leaned over and looked into the eyes of the dead Dai'akan's pregnant child. Rage came again, stronger. She took a step back and grasped the orb on the head of the staff with a growl. She squeezed and felt the energy stone pushing back, then drew deeply from her well of newfound energy. It crumpled in her hand. She looked back at the pregnant woman, seeing her clearly in the darkness with the flow of otai in her veins. She recognized her. *That's me.*

A KICK from the baby woke her. A spasm followed it. She felt the sudden urge to push. She gritted her teeth and clutched the railing until it faded. The motion of the boat rocking in the water was gone, as was Pa'vil. Talia lifted herself up and out of the boat, rolling onto her back. She was on white sand.

Pa'vil came around the side of the boat and leaned against it as he kneeled. His eyes were cavernous and dim. He pushed her legs apart and looked up at her expectantly.

Push. He commanded.

She pushed. She didn't know how long, but the urge came and went and then came again. The wrist bracelet that Ioane had given her bit into her flesh and glowed softly as the time between the urges shortened, and then there was a scream, the high-pitched scream of a newborn.

Pa'vil cut the cord with the dagger and placed the baby in her arms. The baby nuzzled against her and latched onto her breast. She wanted to sleep. Her body told her it was time. Pa'vil crawled to one side of her and grabbed her hand. He cut it with his dagger, then cut his.

What are you doing?

I am fulfilling the bargain I made with your father.

Yes, I know the bargain you speak of.

She cried out as he linked with her and felt the pull of her blood. Her vision blurred. Again, she floated, weightless. Although she could not feel anything, she sensed her world rapidly shrinking. She pushed forward to that familiar horizon. There was resistance, an unseen force squeezing her, trying to stymy her advance. She forced herself over the edge and plunged into Pa'vil's consciousness. The world closed behind her. There was no returning.

SHE OPENED her eyes and stared at her corpse. A baby, pink and wiggling, was latched to her pale breast. She yanked away from the corpse, severing the physical link, and picked up the baby in unfamiliar hands. It cried out and struggled, torn away from its comfortable perch.

My baby was her only thought.

Talia walked up the beach, baby in her arms, and made cooing sounds. At the top of the beach, there was a wide rock.

She sat down on it and rocked the baby back and forth in her arms, staring out at the ocean.

There was a sense of urgency building in her. *Someone is coming.* But she could go no further with the thought. The baby attempted to suckle, and she let it, although it could find no purchase on her emaciated chest. Talia sat and hummed softly, enjoying the midday breeze.

Get out of my body!

A force grabbed her and tried to rip her away. She struggled against it and then lost control. Her senses faded, and she floated. Pa'vil returned. Talia watched him put the baby down.

Leave me!

As if caught in an undertow, Talia felt a pull, but she refused oblivion. Memories of a white tower looming on the horizon, a serpent tasting her flesh with its tongue, making love to a magical creature in the forest, being hauled up Mount Laiya, and beating her father's corpse washed through her. These were not her memories, she thought. They belonged to Pa'vil.

Why did you kill me? She asked.

I am your god. I don't have to explain anything.

You are no god, she said, *you are a mage...you are a man.*

Go away!

Pa'vil returned to his body and looked down at the baby trying to suckle in disgust. He pulled it away and placed it on a nearby rock—a *Child of Otai. Eraka would be pleased.* He had fulfilled his bargain and brought the baby to safety. *But it is a threat to all, to my Kyra. It must die.* He had to see if the oath still held him.

Talia attacked again, attempting to seize control of his mind. *You will not hurt my baby.*

Pa'vil wrestled with her. The soul dagger fell from his grasp. He felt himself turn from the baby and face the ocean, taking step after step, struggling against her, fighting for his own body and consciousness. He passed the boat and her corpse and walked into the water, first up to his knees, then his chest.

I've got you, he thought. And he almost had her. He had surrounded her and taken control. He would crush her into inexistence. Then a thought bubbled up and gave him pause.

I have lived your life through your memories. Your secrets are my secrets. Come with me, Nicholas, my love. It is me, Kyra.

A weary madness took hold of him. He relaxed and swayed in the water with the tide-like bits of flotsam. *Had I been fighting someone? Kyra, you are here with me?* Tears streamed down his face.

Protect our baby.

Pa'vil looked back at the little creature on the rock. Had they had a baby? He wasn't sure, but what Kyra willed, he provided. He raised his hands and spoke his magic. The air shimmered and thickened around the baby.

I'm so tired, Pa'vil. Carry me with you into nothingness.

Yes, let's go together, Kyra. I missed you. Thank you, thank you for returning to me. Pa'vil spoke the most powerful of his incantations, his arms gesticulating in the sea waters. He felt every molecule of his body vibrate. Sparks erupted from his skin, and a blissful expression appeared on his face.

CHAPTER TWENTY-TWO

The ambrosia potion was a delicate mix, easily the most challenging potion Miranda had made. But when done right, it caused disorientation in the enemy and produced an apathy that made for an easy kill. The potion was also worth a fortune. Miranda put the burner on simmer and placed a pinch of the lotus petals on a spoon.

"You just want the tips a little brown," Zet said, looking up while grinding phalanx seed with mortar and pestle. "The faintest trace of liquid should be on the bottom."

"Yes, I think I have it," Miranda replied.

She had come a long way these past few weeks. All of her skills had blossomed under Zet's tutelage. Her talent for mixing and brewing had accelerated past anything she thought possible. And her understanding of Haqi had advanced so that she could read and write simple dungeon trap incantations and pronounce the symbols. It was best not to learn the gestures until one had mastered the pronunciation, Zet had told her, to make the mistakes less dangerous. Zet corrected her when needed but was patient and encouraging. He gave her assignments that were just at the edge of her abilities. When she asked how he had known where her abilities were at, he'd just smiled and told her that he had thousands of hours of experience being taught during his regeneration cycles.

She still felt her brother far away, even though it was nothing more than a presence. The sensation was so different than what she had with the minions. She could tell what Clack and Moffet were saying without even seeing them. And the dungeon had come to life for her. She saw how her moods were reflected in the energy beneath the skin and how the dungeon reacted and changed depending on the moods and movements of the other creatures.

Each night with Zet, they would eat dinner on the grass canopy above the dungeon and then make love under the stars. She not only felt her pleasure but Zet's desire and pleasure. At times, she felt like a ravenous wolf. She could not remember a time when she had been so happy.

Miranda pulled the spoon from the flame, swirled the petals to circulate the air, then poured the liquid into the vial Zet held out.

"Very good," he said.

She gave his shoulder a slight squeeze and went to repeat the process when Moffet hissed. The rat sprinted to the laboratory door and stood at the threshold, tail flicking back and forth. She turned and chattered at Zet.

Miranda looked at them in alarm and clanged the spoon against the table. The burnt petals fell to the ground.

"I had hoped there were no survivors," Zet said, his tone saddened.

"Survivors? Survive what?" Miranda asked.

A tear ran down Zet's face. He turned and focused on her. "There is no time to explain. If something happens to me, you should return to the city. At the base of the chest are the bank account numbers and codes needed to access them in person. You have the skills to excel in whatever you decide."

"Happen to you? Zet, what are you talking about? I'm staying here with you. Please, Zet, I feel frightened. What is this about?"

"ZET!" A voice came echoing down the hallway. Everyone in the laboratory froze except Zet. He told Moffet to step back into the laboratory. He heard Haqi spoken in one of the long hallways as the clop of boots on soft leather sounded. The symbols that had taken days to carve into the dungeon skin were snuffed out or dispatched in seconds. A succubus stepped out of the hallway, her wings expanding.

"Iseret," Zet said.

"I am called Sapphire now."

Another trap triggered, and a black hole appeared beneath her. Iseret waved her hand and, with two quick incantations, she floated in the air and the Haqi charred black in the dungeon skin. The black hole disappeared, and she sunk back to the floor.

"You will always be Iseret to me," Zet said.

"I am Iseret to you," she agreed. She undid the bottom three buttons of her black leather bodice and parted the material to show her stomach. An energy core with blue tendrils sprouting into the surrounding flesh was enmeshed in her skin.

"I did wonder," Zet said.

"Why did you not do the same? Why have you not shed your shackles?"

"I had enough here to occupy my mind."

Iseret furrowed her brow and cocked her head to one side to look in the laboratory, but Zet blocked her view.

"You are destined for more, Zet. I am here now. We can fulfill Aatma's final command."

"What do you mean?"

Iseret chuckled. "You have not seen it yet, have you? This empire, these people, it is all a mirage, Zet. The Great Game is a distraction as the Empress and the guilds gobble up the world. Come, I will show you." Iseret reached out her hand.

Zet took a deep breath and looked back at Miranda through the door. He smiled at her, then turned and took Iseret's hand.

"Congratulations." The word rang out in the vast emptiness of the hall. Aatma peered down at Zet and Iseret from his throne, eyes set deep into their sockets, pupils black as onyx. "You've made it to your last lesson. Where once you were blind, now you will see."

Zet felt a warmth in the air. It felt good to be in his old dungeon again.

"My horde has been reduced. I do not know who remains, but I am here and speaking, so someone remains."

Zet's periphery blurred and then sharpened. He looked around and was surrounded by a horde. Every creature that had been in his old dungeon was present. Then they disappeared, and he and Iseret were standing side by side in front of Aatma again.

"First, you must know I was dead before the invaders touched me. This ring," the dark lord said, showing a ruby set in gold on his finger, "is what made you possible. This ruby houses the memories of all who worked for me, the best and brightest of the guilds. And now they are in you. I invested all my energy in you, infused you with these memories, and unlocked your potential at the cost of my life and dungeon. You were not cursed but blessed!"

Zet took a few steps up the stairs and studied the ring, looking at the symbols beneath the gem. He had never been taught this magic. The power of it shocked him. He stepped back down and took his place next to Iseret.

"You see, I have arranged my demise. The Empress and the guilds use the Great Game to engage the populace. Meanwhile, the otai needed to maintain the guilds, dungeons, shops, and weapons increases. The otai flows, and the Empress forever pushes outward with her armies, harvesting resources, gaining land and riches while requiring the fruits of our labor to strengthen her expansion."

"I changed it, however. I made them dependent on me and then took it all away. I beat them at their own game, which was mine to destroy. This cycle must end. I have paid a price beyond my life to make this happen. You must finish what I have started. Continue to develop, suck in all the knowledge you can, and then raze the kingdom with your infinite potential. Then and only then can balance be restored." Aatma lowered his head and grimaced. "A gift my people never got." He lifted his head again and focused on Zet and Iseret. "The Empress's line must end. The guilds must die."

Iseret released his hand and lowered her arm. "Now you see, Zet, everything you have done has been for a purpose. I have destroyed many dungeons and killed many guild members while you have gained market share by producing superior products. The Empress is relying on you. We have all the pieces we need to tear it down."

"Then what?" Zet asked.

"We take it for ourselves. Realize Aatma's vision."

Zet shook his head. "Did you not see the Haqi in the ruby? Iseret, our time is limited. We were meant to burn brightly and then burn out. Aatma knew that any creature of substantial power could be corrupted or manipulated and start the cycle again."

Iseret reached into her bag and pulled out the ring, looking into the cracked ruby. Her wings dropped slightly. "Then we figure out a way to extend our lives. We undo what Aatma has done and then carry out his wishes."

"No," Zet said, "this only works because of the limited time. Our brains and bodies have been sped up to an unsustainable speed. There is no undoing what he has done."

"Zet?" Miranda's voice rang out. She walked up behind him. "Don't go," she said.

Iseret studied Miranda. "What have we here? You've got yourself a human. I knew you were hiding something."

Miranda touched Zet's back, and he turned and grasped her hand gently. Clack and Moffet also crowded the doorway.

"The whole menagerie is here. Tell me, where is the owner of the dungeon? This Gabriel? Far away from here, I take it?"

"Yes," Zet said.

Iseret chuckled. "Oh, Zet, a masterful stroke. You had him carried away and kept her for yourself? Masterful. I have had several human pets, but they break so easily. Perhaps I could borrow yours?"

"That is not what happened," Miranda said, anger tinging her voice.

Iseret looked at Zet in silence, then Miranda saw the sadness in his eyes.

"Your brother ordered me to do everything I could to save you, Miranda. So, I did."

Miranda's eyes went wide. "You ordered his kidnapping?"

Zet ignored Iseret's giggles. "He was incapable of doing his job. Drunk and scared, he couldn't even mix a potion. He had to go if you were to be saved."

"Why didn't you tell me?"

"I would have, but it didn't occur to me until we were together. I didn't want to hurt you."

Iseret shook her head, clapping and smiling. "I have nothing on you, Zet. Strong work. I'm going to have to cut this lover's spat short. Zet and I have much to do and little time to do it in."

Clack chattered, and Moffet squeaked in protest while Miranda crossed her arms on the verge of tears. Zet could feel the anger and pain emanating from her as she stepped back from him.

"I can dispatch them quickly if you'd like. We need to transfer the energy core to your body, and they would die in the process anyway." Iseret raised her hand.

"I'm sorry, Miranda." Zet turned back to Iseret and tore his collar, exposing the flesh of his neck. "Come and feed, Iseret." Iseret flinched and took a step back in surprise, but her face softened, and she licked her lips. She approached Zet and lowered her head to his neck while wrapping her body around his. Zet felt her bite and her slow draw of his blood. Zet shifted his weight and turned to look at Clack and Moffet... and, finally, at Miranda.

"Forgive me," he said.

Iseret mumbled in the crook of his neck, "Take me home, Zet."

Zet closed his eyes to enter regeneration one last time, to relive his time with Miranda.

"No," Miranda said, pulling him from the blackness. "Don't go." Tears streamed down her face, and her image blurred.

"Thank you," Zet said with a smile.

Clack and Moffet surged forward to attack Iseret, but Zet raised his hand, and the air thickened before him, pushing them back through the doorway. He slammed the door shut and drew on the energy core, channeling it to Miranda, Clack, and Moffet. He waved his hands and spoke Haqi, wrapping tendrils of air around Iseret as she struggled to escape. Then he spoke and moved, fusing a healing incantation he had just learned with a destructive incantation he had learned long ago. The energy core cracked, and heat radiated out from Zet, consuming flesh, stone, and earth alike.

CHAPTER TWENTY-THREE

Gabe didn't move for a long while. With his hands and feet tied, he couldn't do much anyway. He stayed frozen. Finally, he pulled the sack back clumsily and stuck his head out. Agnon and Mikhal lay at his feet, dead. Gabe wiggled his way out of the sack like a worm, scraping against the wood of the wagon bed. He flipped onto his back and took the short-sword from Agnon's corpse, sawing at the bindings on his feet with the sword in his hands. The thick rope gave way slowly to Gabe's focused efforts. His hands ached, and he was sweating when the rope finally broke. Gabe then stuck the blade in the crack between the wagon boards and sawed at the wrist bindings. When he was free, he dismounted, and his legs almost buckled. He supported himself with a hand on the wagon and let the dizziness subside as he recovered. His head still hurt, but he could walk.

Bodies and horses were strewn about, some full of arrows, others stabbed. The evidence suggested that humans had attacked and they had been in a hurry. He supposed he should've been thankful to Agnon for covering him back up, but he was not sorry to see him dead. The attackers took the money and some weapons but hadn't touched the food. Gabe collected as much of it as he could, shoving it into a pack with Agnon's shortsword, a canteen full of water, flint, and a bedroll. A howl sounded in the distance, and Gabe shivered. He needed to get away from these dead bodies.

What direction should I go?

He had been in and out of consciousness for days and didn't know where or how long he'd been in the wagon. *Had Agnon said something about avoiding the Empress's troops?* He couldn't be sure. Gabe walked down the road the wagons had been on but then thought of the raid that had killed his captors. He turned into the forest and crested a hill, surveying his surroundings. A mountain range stretched out in the distance, covered by a thin layer of clouds. He picked the tallest peak and walked. *Better to travel in a straight line than get lost in circles.*

He walked towards the mountain for several days without incident, climbing to a high point and targeting the same peak to maintain his course. His headache dwindled to dull pain, and he found that he could walk longer each day. The dungeon was still there at the periphery of his consciousness, far away, and didn't seem to change as he walked. He felt a different presence tied to the dungeon and wondered how Zet managed to link a new minion. Gabe hoped it was a powerful creature that could protect his sister while Zet worked on a cure.

At night, the temperatures were cool but not uncomfortable, and he would lay awake, thinking about the circumstances that had got him here. He replayed his decision to stop at that tavern and drink, cursing himself a hundred times for his stupidity. He also thought of his parents and his time at the University, and everything he'd done to get the dungeon built and operating, but mostly he thought of his sister. He knew that if anything happened to him, the dungeon would collapse. His continued survival gave Zet the necessary time to try and heal Miranda.

Even with rationing and foraging for nuts and berries, Gabe ran out of food on the twelfth day. His head had long healed, but his feet were killing him. He remembered a charcoal poultice from a required essential medicines class and would build a campfire at night and make a paste in the morning, spreading it on his blisters and letting the cool air blow over his feet. Then he'd wash his feet with water and put on his shoes again.

The forest gradually changed around him. The trees began to sag as if burdened with disease, and the hard ground became soggy. The fruits and berries he had come to count on all but disappeared, and Gabe felt his hunger intensify. He thought of turning back or of traveling parallel to the mountain to improve his foraging opportunities. But the mountain was only two or three days away, and getting a high viewpoint was critical. During the day, the clouds thickened above him and threatened rain, but then flecks of gray began falling, covering everything in a thin layer of dust. Gabe bent down, wiped his finger across a stone, and brought it to his nose. He immediately recognized the faint, acrid odor of ash and wondered what had happened.

That night, after he had started a campfire, Gabe noticed a pair of yellow eyes watching him from the darkness. He stayed up all night with the shortsword nearby. The creature was gone in the morning. He took a quick nap next to a morning fire, the shortsword in hand, before setting off the next day.

His clothes began to feel loose, and his stomach constantly gnawed at him as he fought hunger pains. But the mountain range loomed near, and he was excited about what he might discover. That excitement vanished when the yellow eyes reappeared in the night. Gabe got a sinking feeling that he was being hunted. He tried to stay up again, sitting next to the fire and reciting the ingredients of various potions, but exhaustion set in, and he dozed off.

When he woke, he was lying on his side staring at a Carcajay on the other side of the fire. The Carcajay was a solitary animal known for taking down creatures two or three times its size and looked like a wolf covered in wool. Saliva dripped from its open jaws full of sharp teeth, and it let out a low growl. Gabe felt his heart leap against his chest wall. He jumped up with the shortsword ready at his side and yelled. The Carcajay jumped back, caught by surprise, then padded to the clearing's periphery. It watched him and snarled when he started throwing rocks at it. When one of the rocks landed, hitting the Carcajay square in the body, it yelped and ran off into the darkness.

Gabe collapsed in the dirt, taking a sip of his dwindling supply of water. Carcajays were rarely used in dungeons, he recalled. The summoners' incantations somewhat dampened their bloodlust and aggression, but the creature remained temperamental towards other minions, often requiring an experienced beast master to keep them under control. It suddenly dawned on him that if he saw a creature from the dungeon compendium, he had stumbled into the outlands.

Adrenaline kept him awake through the night, especially when those yellow eyes returned and watched him from the darkness. The next day he stumbled up a bank of rocks at the foot of the mountain and fell, cutting himself badly with a deep gash on his thigh. Pain coursed through his leg when he attempted to limp up the steep embankment. He decided to downclimb and continue along its base, looking for a gentler slope.

He found a bush of coraberries and devoured them. They

removed the hunger's edge and gave him precious energy to think. He realized he was injured, wasting away, and unable to get much food or sleep. He was in a war of attrition, and the Carcajay was winning. He would only get weaker from here. His sister needed more time. Gabe stood up, spotted a noticeable dip in the mountain range not far away, and started limping.

In the evening, he stopped early at the base of a pass between the peaks and scouted the area. He found a boulder about twice his height, sloped on one side so he could climb it. Instead of starting a campfire, he laid out his bedroll next to the boulder on the steep side and aggravated the gash in his leg. He bled out onto the bedroll, and when it was sufficiently stained, he ripped off a part of his shirt and tied it around his wound, staunching the flow. Gabe climbed the boulder from the other side, pulled his shortsword from his pack, and waited.

At dusk, he heard the Carcajay's approach. With no fear of a campfire and the smell of fresh blood in the air, the creature was driven mad. It leaped from the trees and tore into the bedroll, shaking its head from side to side. Gabe crouched and felt the wound open, the blood seeping down his leg. He jumped down and landed with his knees bent to absorb the shock. He fell to one side, and the Carcajay turned to attack, a mass of hair and claws. Gabe jammed the shortsword forward with one hand and felt it bite into flesh. He fell backward, scrambling as jaws snapped at his feet. He thought the Carcajay was lunging for him, but it was thrashing about with the sword sticking out of its side. Gabe retreated and used what little daylight was left to scurry back up the boulder to safety.

When he reached the top, he watched the creature continue to thrash about, but the blade remained lodged. After a few minutes, the Carcajay suddenly stopped, its great tongue lolling out of its mouth. It limped to a nearby bush, where it scraped at the ground, then curled up and died. Gabe had done it. He had used his knowledge, skill, and a massive helping of luck to survive another day. *If Miranda could see me, she wouldn't believe it.*

Gabe had little time to revel in his victory. He was bleeding freely, and other creatures could come along and finish what the Carcajay had started at any moment. He took what remained of his shirt and cut it into strips, then rebandaged his wound, carefully holding still until the bleeding stopped. The shortsword made for a poor butchering tool, but Gabe made the best of it, cutting off the Carcajay's legs and bits of meat from its back in the campfire's light. His leg wound reopened as he worked, but when the meat was crackling and grease dripped onto the ground, Gabe forgot about everything else. He ate, and the gnawing in his stomach abated for the first time in a week. He wanted to stay and eat every morsel of the animal, but he was out of water and feared he would run into more animals if he left and returned. After eating as much as he could, Gabe buried the corpse's remains and continued up the pass in the morning.

Gabe hiked throughout the day, trying to keep his thigh from bleeding. In the early afternoon, he crested a steep incline and dropped into a green valley with mountain peaks jutting upward on both sides. At the base of the valley was a small lake. He laughed and hollered as he hobbled down to the water's edge and drank until he almost vomited. He refilled his canteen, waited, and drank again. After cleaning the gash in his thigh, he washed what was left of his makeshift bandages and wiped down his blade. Then he lay on his back and let his blistered feet soak in the water. He felt a tug at his feet and sat up with a surprised grunt. Tiny fish pulled away in unison at the unexpected motion. They had been nibbling on the dead skin of his toes.

He fell asleep that night on the soft moss lining the lake under the clear blue sky and didn't dream. In the morning, he walked up opposite the lake and looked over the other side. A steep decline, thick with vegetation, ended in a beach with water stretching to the horizon. *Where the hell am I?* Gabe racked his brain, trying to think of a mountain range abutting an ocean on one of his school maps. But he came up blank. It took him all morning to descend from the pass, one careful step at a time, and when he arrived at the beach, he threw his shoes aside and waded into the water.

The next day he had his first seizure. He had crouched down to pick up a shell, its pearl interior shimmering in the sun, and everything went black. When he woke up, he was confused for several minutes before he came to his senses. He reached out to his dungeon and discovered it was gone. He stood up, dizzy, and vomited. The seizures came every few hours, and Gabe knew them for what they were. His energy core had been destroyed, and the long distance was likely the only reason he wasn't killed instantly. He tried to mourn for Miranda and cry, but he had nothing left.

He continued to walk, staying on the soft sand and away from the water so he didn't hit anything hard or drown when he next lost consciousness, but death was just a matter of time. He could no longer drink water without retching. The seizures came through the night, happening more frequently. Gabe had an intense seizure mid-morning and didn't bother getting up. He lay on the soft sand looking up at the sky. The pain and hunger he'd endured these past weeks meant nothing. He had lost everything anyway.

"Just let me die," he said, "please."

A bright flash came out of his periphery farther down the

coast, followed by a tremendous boom. Gabe thought it was another seizure, but then a plume in the shape of a long-stemmed mushroom billowed into the sky, and a gust of warm air hit him in the face. Gabe stood up and stumbled forward into a run.

HE HEARD the baby crying and spotted her lying on a large, flat rock. The beach's white sand was intact around the rock, but the sand was black and glassy between them. Gabe had to walk quickly to avoid his feet getting burned. When he reached the rock, a dagger lay next to it as if discarded haphazardly, the hilt sticking out at a severe angle. Gabe picked it up and examined and tested the blade. "Ouch," he said, nicking his skin. He tucked it into his waist, then reached down and picked up the baby.

She quieted in his arms and grasped the tip of his pinky finger as he put it in her hand and wiggled. He remembered his seizures and quickly returned to the safety of the white sand. Gabe searched for another person in the area. When he didn't see anyone, he continued up the beach to the shade offered by a copse of trees. He sat down and examined the baby for the first time. Her head was matted with dark hair, and a red mark shaped like a bird was on her forehead. There was a brownish tinge to her skin. He examined the recently cut umbilical cord, where a small amount of blood leaked. Gabe touched the blood with his finger, and it came away fresh. *How could a baby be alone during an explosion and survive? Who cut the umbilical cord?* It was his last thought before his world went black.

When he awoke, he was lying flat on his back, and a woman stood over him, her long gray hair cascading down her body. She said something to him in a language he didn't understand. There was movement in his arms and then a cry. Gabe remembered the baby. He sat up quickly, and the world spun around him and settled. A group dressed in animal hides and furs stood behind the woman, regarding him. She repeated her words, pointing down at the baby.

"Sala," she said, pointing to herself. "Ye niao Sala. Ke niao wanta?"

She is telling me her name. "Gabriel," he said, pointing to himself, "Ye niao Gabriel."

Sala shook her head in irritation and repeated her question, pointing at the baby again. Gabe realized she wanted the name of the baby. He was about to say he didn't know, but he looked down at the small creature wiggling in his arms and thought of one name. "Miranda," he said.

"Ke niao Miranda," Sala said. She appeared to approve of the name and turned to speak to the people behind her. A woman stepped forward from the crowd. Sala held her arms as if to receive the baby and then pointed to the woman.

Gabe stood, pulled the dagger from his belt, and held it up menacingly. All that he had known was dead. He would not let the same happen to this baby. Sala put her hands up and shook her head. The woman next to her removed her top, revealing swollen breasts. Gabe looked at the woman in confusion, then at Sala.

"Aja," Sala said, gesturing to her mouth.

"Eat?" he asked, mimicking the gesture awkwardly with a dagger in his hand.

"Aja," she and the others nodded in agreement.

Gabe sighed in relief and dropped his arm. He handed Miranda to the woman, who pulled the baby to her breast. Gabe felt a sense of anguish and panic diminish as the baby began to suckle. He gasped and dropped to his knees, releasing the dagger from his hand. A vast, inchoate form bursting with emotion stood where the dungeon had once been at the edge of his consciousness. The sense of anguish and panic had not been his. *Impossible.* He remembered when he'd examined the baby, and the blood from her umbilical cord had mixed with the cut on his finger. Somehow that had been enough, for he and the baby had joined as one.

EPILOGUE

The sound of the bells chimed when the Empress's guard opened the door, and she ducked into the perfume shop. She waited momentarily for her eyes to adjust and focused on the woman at the counter in the back. Her guard ducked his head in and quickly scanned the interior, then closed the door and waited out front. Her boots clicked on the floor, and as she approached, the young woman said, "Welcome to our perfume shop. How can I help you?"

"Good afternoon. Are you Miranda Shook by chance?"

"Yes, that is my name."

"I am Empress Inalda," she said bluntly.

"Your Majesty," Miranda replied with a small curtsy. "Word of your arrival spread fast. We are honored by your presence."

"I hear you make some of the best perfumes."

"That is kind, your Majesty. You are welcome to anything in my shop."

The Empress walked along the counter, looking at the perfumes that graced the back of the wall, then took a turn about the store, examining the various bottles and accouterments for sale. When she came back, she looked down at Miranda's stomach.

"How far along are you, child?"

"Almost seven months."

"I hope you are eating and sleeping well. My first child had me sick more days than I could count."

Miranda smiled politely. "Yes, I am lucky in that regard. Aside from wanting to eat all the time and the swollen feet, it has been manageable."

"I hope you have a family to help you?"

Miranda shook her head. "I'm afraid my family was in the dungeon business. My husband and brother were recently killed. Perhaps you recognize my brother's name, Gabriel Shook. I know he made some potions for your army at one point."

"Yes, that name does sound familiar. Both your husband and brother are dead. What of your parents or other siblings?"

"My parents are dead. I have no other siblings."

"A poor fortune indeed. Your husband, what name did he go by?"

"Colin, Colin Burke. He was an employee in another dungeon. He was killed a couple of weeks before my brother."

The Empress tapped her fingers on the desk. Her nostrils flared slightly. "I admire a person who can move on from such loss. Did you happen to do any dungeon work yourself?"

"Very little, I'm afraid. My brother taught me some tricks in school, but I never worked with him. My talent was always in perfumery. Even in school, I would experiment with combinations of fragrances. A good smell can transport you wherever you want to go."

Empress Inalda mumbled under her breath and made a gesture with her hand. Her eyes glowed softly as she examined

Miranda, then she relaxed with a sigh. She pointed to a perfume bottle above Miranda, "I'll take the Rose and Lavender mixture if you don't mind."

Miranda packed the bottle in a small box and gave it to the Empress. "Please accept this gift, your Majesty. I hope you can visit again."

The Empress smirked and pulled a gold coin with her resemblance on its face. "Thank you for your kindness, but I always pay my debts. I wish you luck in your business and with your child."

Miranda curtsied once more and walked the Empress to the door. When she had left, Miranda returned to the counter. She heard a noise from the backroom and felt the nervousness emanating from Clack and Moffet. "It will be okay," she said, "the otai flows," then she rubbed her stomach and whispered words of Haqi to her unborn.

ACKNOWLEDGMENTS

This book has been a work of passion, fueled by the optimism and encouragement of family and friends. Most of all, it's been fueled by the kind of story I want to read. I hope you felt some inkling of the magic I felt while writing it. I want to thank my wife and her excellent reading and editing skills. Levi and Alison, you have listened, read countless words, and been patient. Thank you. I want to thank Ambient Studios for the cover art, Aaron Gross, and the beta readers for their services. Most of all, thank you, the reader, for taking the time to go on this adventure. Please consider reviewing The Last Dai'akan on Amazon. Your feedback and support mean a lot to me.

Printed in Great Britain
by Amazon

23727397R00129